Spruce Lake

Arabell Spencer

Copyright © 2024 Arabell Spencer

All rights reserved

The characters and events portrayed in this book are fictitious. Any similarity to real persons, living or dead, is coincidental and not intended by the author.

No part of this book may be reproduced, or stored in a retrieval system, or transmitted in any form or by any means, electronic, mechanical, photocopying, recording, or otherwise, without express written permission of the publisher.

Chapter 1

"Thanks, Willow. I know the timing of the orders has been tricky lately."

I looked at Lanie across the register and smiled. "You've had your hands a little full."

She patted the baby she had strapped around her with a sling and nodded her head. At her side, six-year-old Benji chimed in. "Mom got all the new orders done last night. I helped. Baby Kayla was crying a lot, but I helped and we got it done, right Mom?" Benji hopped from foot to foot and looked up adoringly at his mom.

"That we did, buddy."

I looked on and felt so happy for my friend. Not long ago, she'd walked into the County Food Cooperative I manage as a nervous new employee at a local farm buying groceries for the farm meals she prepared for their crew. Now, just a few short years later, she had married the farmer, become mom to his little boy, and had a baby of her own. And she was an incredibly talented local foods caterer who supplied my store with premade food for sale. The things she was doing with a baby strapped to her blew my mind - and she was ridiculously happy doing all of it.

I tried hard to not let the impatient man in line behind her rush our interaction. She was comfortable around me now, but she was shy, and I didn't want him making her feel uncomfortable. I was covering the register because one of my regular cashiers had called in sick and the other was on break. Mr. Impatient would just have to wait.

As we finished putting her groceries in her cloth bags and loading them into her basket, we said a heartfelt goodbye.

Then I had to actually look at Mr. Impatient who stood before me. Great, I thought, inwardly rolling my eyes. Another tourist... I knew they were good for business – for everyone in the community. Good for the local economy. But they really tried my patience.

This one was no exception. He had nearly every high-end ingredient we carried on the belt ready to check out. Whereas Lanie's order consisted of whole foods and staples, this guy had a pile of specialty, prepared foods. True, we only carried minimally processed, locally made prepared foods, and, true, I bought my share of those items, but still.

He cleared his throat, and I shifted my gaze from his purchases up to his eyes. In contrast to the locals who usually came to the store in Dickies and hoodies, he had on slim fitting tan pants and a white button-down, peeking out from a light blue quarter zip sweater. He *looked* expensive. The sweater brought out intense blue eyes that were startling against his slightly tanned complexion and, but for some salty pieces, nearly black hair. He was gorgeous. No surprise there. Money often did that to people. All the grooming. All the time.

In our small Maine town, we had our share of hipsters, lumberjack beards, emo kids, and goth preteens. But they usually didn't stick around. Once they got to be eighteen or so, they usually left the area – for college or just better opportunities. Mostly what was left was a group of regular people. In this area, that meant farmers, teachers, small business owners, and people who just had everyday jobs. This guy was not regular people.

"Did you find everything you needed?" I asked robotically and started scanning his purchases.

"I did. Thank you," he responded. I had to admit that he responded politely. Not always a given with these people. And I guess he didn't really seem impatient. More... eager? He had an open expression and looked ready to engage. And why wouldn't he feel eager? Life was good for this guy.

"Did you need bags for your purchases?" I asked, frustrated with his type for ignoring our recently passed state law that discouraged one-time use bags.

"I saw the sign, so I added some," he said, indicating the most expensive reusable bags we carried, stacked neatly at the end of his order.

"Great." Of course, he would buy a stack of those...

"I was wondering," he said with a friendly (phony tourist) smile affixed to his face, "who I would need to speak to about some wholesale possibilities."

"Wholesale?" I asked, surprised and even more irritated. "We don't do wholesale." I lifted my eyes to his face and saw he was waiting for more. "The only step closer to wholesale than us," I grudgingly continued, "is dealing directly with the farmers and food producers." I was never myself with these privileged visitors, but I was almost always able to maintain a façade of pleasantry. This question ran the risk of cracking my already compromised civility. "A food Co-op is a place for farmers and customers to intersect," I said. "We're not a supplier."

He looked at me skeptically, like he thought I didn't understand what he wanted. "Okay, gotcha."

I finished ringing him up, gave him his total, and started to put his items in his new bags while he dealt with the card reader.

"Any recommendations for local restaurants?" he asked me as I was finishing up.

"Take a walk along main street and take your pick," I retorted. "They all have their strong points." I knew I wasn't being very nice, but really, could he stop with the chattiness already? As if, in this community, I would declare a favorite. All the small businesses had to work together – even if I thought the most popular seafood restaurant was awful, I wasn't going to say that out loud in the store.

"I like Cupie's," Nancy Landry said, inserting herself in the conversation. She was the customer behind Mr. Eager in line. There were two others waiting behind her now as well. I really wanted to move this along.

"Cupie's is good," George Dimov said from behind Nancy, "but Full Plate is my favorite."

The man in front of me turned to the customers behind him and graciously thanked them, promising to check out both eateries.

He picked up his bags and looked at me, still smiling but with a curious look on his face as well. "Thanks for your help," he said. "See you next time."

I was thankful when Brendan was able to come in to cover for the sick cashier later that day. He was my newest manager – recently promoted. I still wasn't convinced I'd made the right decision with his promotion – he was young and not always the most reliable. But I was relieved he was here today.

As soon as he got in, I grabbed some coffee from the store's small café nook and settled myself in the tiny office in the back of the store. I had quarterly financial reports that needed some attention before a meeting with Ruthie on Monday to review them. Ruthie was our board president, the closest thing I had to a mentor, and she had recently insisted I stop working on weekends. As Head of Operations, I wasn't really supposed to work weekends anyway, but something always seemed to come up. Anyway, if I was going to stick to the new resolution to not work this weekend, I needed to finish these reports before I left today.

Another reason to not work this weekend - my birthday was on Sunday. I wasn't really a birthday person. I always kept the date to myself because it just made me uncomfortable. Like asking people to make a big deal out of you just because you were born – weird to me. I would go to my parents on Saturday night for dinner. Mom would make a chocolate cake. And I planned to treat myself to a solo hike on Sunday. I was turning thirty-two, so while I didn't see a need for celebration, I did need to do some processing.

Finding yet another correction that needed to be made in the reports, I startled, suddenly remembering on top of everything else, I had a date later that night. I forced myself to focus even harder to power through the rest of my work.

I was in the same position, hunched over the computer, into the evening. I peeled myself out of the old office chair ten minutes before I was supposed to meet Chris for dinner. The afternoon had not gone well – multiple interruptions from vendors and workers, a printer problem, and a clogged toilet in the bathroom that apparently no one could sort out but me. The reports were done but not perfect, and I worried Ruthie would grill me on Monday.

But I had promised Chris we would meet up, and I knew my tired eyes, mind, and body weren't going to make much more progress tonight. I released my long brown hair from the top knot I had tied it into, combed through it with my fingers, and stretched as much as I could in the small room, my five-foot-eight frame and long limbs not really having enough space. As I always did, I stretched like I remembered stretching when I was little, warming up in my ballet classes. Also, as always, I felt a twinge of regret for all the things that had not come to be in my life.

I shook the feeling off, looking down at my work clothes, which consisted of dark wash jeans and a white bohemian top. It would have to do for the evening. It was casual anyway. We were meeting up at Black Dog – my favorite local place, not that I would ever tell Mr. Eager that. It was unpretentious local food – grass-fed burgers, local potatoes fried in lard, cheesecake from Smith's Farm ingredients. They added in some local veggies for salads to lighten things up a little. But it was friendly, relaxed. The kind of place I felt comfortable in. The kind of place Mr. City Pants would probably look down his nose at.

Jeez, why was I still thinking about that guy? We had tourists in and out of this place all the time. I noticed and moved on. Stoneton, our small town, was a popular spot because of its proximity to the Maine coastline as well as lots of lakefront property. We had three lakes within five miles of the small but quaint downtown, and it was a short drive to the beach. It allowed local businesses to thrive, including the Co-op, several restaurants, coffee shops, a bookstore, and some small boutiques. It was a smaller, crunchier, and, in my humble opinion, better version of the bigger, nearby college town of Beecham.

I made the short walk to Black Dog and considered whether this thing I had going with Chris was going to work out. We'd been seeing each other for a few months, but I was keeping him at arm's length. If he was willing to keep things casual, it would be perfect. I'd had three relationships since finishing high school. They had all ended *carefully* – meaning I had tried to extricate myself in a way that would keep the friendships intact. Three times taught me that was really difficult, and I didn't want to repeat history with Chris. I had accepted that I was a casual kind of woman. If someone started getting serious – talking about the future or even love, it was kind of the beginning of the end for me. I couldn't imagine tying my life to someone else's in that way. The older I got, the less appealing it was. I needed to find someone who felt similarly, and I was starting to fear that wasn't Chris.

He stood up as soon as I walked into the restaurant and greeted me with a kiss on the cheek. "You look amazing, Willow," he said. "You always do."

I laughed at him. "I'm not sure flattery works on me. You know I came straight from work."

"Where you looked amazing," he tossed back, smiling.

I had known Chris for a few years. He ran a company that built floating boat docks. We were about the same age, but he'd grown up in another part of Maine, so we didn't have the long history I'd shared with all of my former boyfriends. I considered this to be a plus in the relationship pro/con list.

"I ordered your usual," he said. "I hope that was okay - I thought you would be hungry since I doubt you ate anything today. Seemed like it was another long day when I got your text that you were coming straight from the store."

"Yes, totally okay. Thanks. I'm starving."

We enjoyed our time together. The food was great, and Chris was a funny guy. He was warm and attractive with sandy blond hair that was always a little shaggy. We kept things pretty surface-level, which suited me just fine.

The awkward part was the end of the evening. Chris invited me to his place as he had for the last several times we'd gone out. I declined as I had each time he'd asked, telling him I had a busy weekend ahead. For a normal couple, we had been going out far too long for me to still be undecided about sleeping with him. He was being patient, trying to go along with my casual approach, but I could tell we were going to need to have *the conversation* soon. I enjoyed going out but didn't want to risk another friendship by turning this into a relationship that I knew wouldn't go anywhere.

As we were headed toward the door and saying our goodbyes, Mr. Eager walked into the restaurant. He took in the place with wide eyes and an easy expression. It irritated me how comfortable he was here. Where were his people? Usually, tourists traveled in packs or pairs. He was probably forty or so. His type usually had a wife and kids in tow. Or, alternatively, business associates if they were doing some sort of work retreat in Maine. I heard him tell the host that he was picking up a takeout order.

"Hello again," he said looking at me with a friendly expression. "Small world."

"Small town," I said.

"Hello," Chris offered, putting his left arm around my back but offering his right to the man to shake. "Chris Adams."

"Anthony Kaplan," Mr. Eager said, happily reaching out to shake Chris's hand. "Good to meet you." Turning to me, he said, "So, is this one your favorite?"

"Place to eat?" Chris asked. "Yeah, Willow loves this place. Good choice, man."

Anthony gave Chris a friendly look, but there was something disapproving in it.

I was annoyed – two men talking about me instead of to me. Well, Anthony had directed his question to me, I guess, but it felt like he was trying to triumph a little in finding me here – as if he'd gotten his question answered even though I hadn't given him a recommendation earlier. And then Chris making sure he marked me as his territory. I think our needed relationship conversation had just been accelerated.

Chapter 2

Happy Birthday to me.

I lay in bed Sunday morning questioning my plan. I had been excited about spending the day hiking, but I wasn't so sure this morning. Now I kind of felt like staying in bed all day and not contemplating the fact that I was another year older.

The night before had taken away the almost zen feeling I'd been embracing leading up to the annual milestone. I knew it was always a time when I looked at my life and considered where I was (or wasn't), but I wasn't expecting to be disappointed or anxious about it. As usual, an evening with my parents resulted in my healthy outlook evaporating into thin air.

Mom had made a chicken and rice casserole, placed on the table in a nine by thirteen dish and scooped onto the old, chipped plates I'd eaten on for as long as I could remember. She then presented me with a one-layer chocolate cake still sitting in another nine by thirteen pan. I think she used a box mix.

I wasn't complaining. Just stating the facts. My mom had always been a full-time homemaker, but she hated cooking. Her goal was to spend as little time at it as possible. She hated thinking about food, shopping for food, or preparing food. It didn't give us a lot to talk about regarding my job where food was the topic of conversation all the time. She did the things expected of her as a homemaker – cleaning the house, cooking the meals, and she worked hard by necessity, having been a farmer's wife – but she spent any free time she could get on her physical appearance and worrying about other people's perceptions.

Things had been fine until we were eating the cake – officially the birthday portion of the evening.

"Willow, I think you need to put yourself out there more. Look at me and your dad," my mom had said expansively. "You just know when it happens. And it will happen to you. But you have to be *open* to it."

This was familiar ground with my mom. She had met my dad when she was only eighteen. She was a beautiful woman even now. I realized long ago that I hadn't inherited her level of beauty. I was fine. Maybe even pretty – at least I'd been told that. But my mom was next level. A little shorter than me but curvier with a catalog model's face. At eighteen, she had easily caught my father's eye and, according to the story, he was persistent in his pursuit. They'd quickly married and been, more or less, happily married since.

"Mom, I'm dating someone now. I'm not *not* putting myself out there. And did you ever think you and dad were just lucky? I'm not sure that happens to everybody."

"Maybe if you just got gussied up a little more often," she said, gesturing around her head as if to show me my hair could really use some attention. "Men like it when a woman takes pains."

"She's fine, Mona. She doesn't care about that stuff." My dad looked at me, nodding his head as if I'd confirmed his statement, then continued. "Critter, did you hear about the new snow blowers we got in at the store? It's a little early for them, but we're close to selling out. They'll throw twenty feet no problem every time. But I think people are going to be mighty upset when we get our first snow. I don't think the drive train is going to perform very good."

"No, Dad. I hadn't heard about it. You can show me next time I'm in the shop."

My dad worked at the local farm and home supply store. It was normal that he was there now, but it's not how I had grown up. This little house we sat in now was very different from the big farmhouse where I'd been raised. And my dad working at a store was certainly different than his work when I was growing up. I'd spent as much time with him out in the fields and with the animals as I had anywhere else. His idea of bonding with me had always been to talk about machinery or some other farming tidbit. Where my mom tried to talk to me about my appearance all the time, my dad tried to plant me in the tomboy-for- life category.

The truth was I'd never been either – never a tomboy but also never a woman focused on securing a man by perfecting her "feminine wiles" (my mom's unfortunate term). I'd just been a girl who needed to help her hard-working dad out. Especially once the farm started to be in trouble financially. For both of my parents that meant tomboy. It was my dad's mission to keep me there and my mom's mission to break me free of it.

What they both accomplished was consistently making me feel worse about myself after spending time with them that I felt before. Their comments made me feel like I was failing at life - too unattractive to experience a magic moment where I met my life partner - and like I was still a child who hadn't figured anything out yet.

Happy Birthday to me.

I lingered, feeling grumpy, a bit longer in bed, dwelling on the night before until Sunshine planted herself on my chest. My happy, orange furball of a cat made herself comfortable and looked at me so pleasantly. It was impossible to not leave the night before behind. Unlike my mom, I wasn't prone to depression. I liked to be happy. Sure, I got frustrated, down, sad, anxious, tired. But I didn't stay there. I'd seen how hard that was growing up with her and was so very thankful I hadn't inherited it. Sunshine, knitting her paws on my chest and giving me the slow blink to greet me on my birthday, was enough to snap me out of it.

"Breakfast?" I asked her as I peeled the covers back. Her ears twitched, and she followed me into the kitchen.

I'd brought home a special pastry from the shop for my birthday breakfast. I turned on the toaster oven and pulled Sunshine's food out of the drawer. She swished around my legs as I put the raspberry galette in the oven, got my coffee going, and put her food out for her.

A bit later, she joined me on my prized possession – my lavender Queen Anne-style sofa - as I enjoyed the morning light and my birthday breakfast. I was generally a minimalist. I had a mix of styles, but what they shared was very little fluff. I couldn't stand excessive layering, ruffling, or stuff – a rebellion against my mom's approach to her appearance. And I couldn't bring myself to spend much money on things – especially after the struggle with the farm. But I had an appreciation for beauty, so the things I did have in my space were things that I loved and that I felt good having around me.

It was another difference from my parents. My mom cared about her physical appearance (and mine), but the feel of things, the look of things in my environment – that wasn't something I grew up with. It was something I first learned to recognize about myself when I took a photography class with Mr. Arsenault my sophomore year in high school. When he taught me about composition and techniques in the darkroom to enhance certain elements, I began to understand how much the beauty around me mattered. How much it influenced my mood. Even my happiness.

That was why I liked solo hikes.

I finished my breakfast, hurriedly got ready to leave the house, and grabbed my camera bag. The day was going to be spent hiking in a state park that had miles of wooded hiking trails, but it was along the coastline, so I would be able to photograph some woodland creatures and look for some interesting shots in and near the water as well. I carried both a digital and film camera. Even though I mostly spent my time working in digital photography now, Mr. Arsenault still allowed me – no, welcomed me – to join him in the high school darkroom from time to time.

Several hours later, I was feeling invigorated from the miles covered and happy about a particularly lovely shot I had gotten of a beaver working on its dam in a little stream at the deepest part of the woods I'd covered. I had packed all my gear into my camera backpack and was about to trek back through the woods to where my car was parked when I saw a runner approaching on the trail. I glanced up to confirm a flash of orange in a nearby tree, and I stepped to the side into the brush to let the runner pass. But, instead of running by me, he slowed to a stop.

"Hello again," Anthony Kaplan greeted in a friendly tone.

He was kitted out in perfectly fitting, top of the line running gear. Fitted dark grey joggers, a lighter grey moisture-wicking half zip hoodie, and bright yellow fancy running shoes. They were so expensive (presumably) that I didn't even recognize the brand.

"Hi," I said, adjusting my backpack and hoping that greeting each other was all it would take to move him along. I looked down at my outfit. I had put on jeans, wool socks with well-worn Birkenstock sandals, and a loose, lightweight tan sweater. Why did I care that he must have thought I looked like a small-town hick? I mean I guess I was, but still.

"Out for a hike?" he asked.

I really didn't like this guy. I hated his easygoing, "you know you love me" attitude. Everything came easily for him, and I had to fight against my inner snarky nature (almost always kept to myself) that would have replied, "It would seem so."

Instead, I considered some of the things I'd meditated on throughout the morning – the fact that being rude to this man made me feel bad. That I didn't like being a jerk, and I needed to stop doing it for myself – not for him or people like him. So, I sucked it up and answered with a simple, "Yes, I am." Then I followed up with, "Just heading back home now." I snuck another peek up into the tree.

I hoped he would get the hint and continue on his way, so I could get home.

"You must be an expert on these woods," he said, smiling even more freely. "Is the green trail or the blue one better? I had a hard time deciding."

"Well, they're both good," I said. "Just depends on what you're looking for."

"Ah," he said, his smile dimming just a touch. "I forgot. You don't like to share your favorites."

I was irritated he had taken it that way. I was trying to be nice to him, trying to treat him like I would anyone else. I wasn't trying to be evasive or dismissive like I had been in the store when I'd met him. And yet, he was taking it that way.

"I'm not sharing a favorite," I said, a little grumpy edge creeping into my tone, "because I don't have a favorite. They're both good trails. It just depends on whether you're in the mood to spend most of your time in the woods or along the water."

"Well, if you don't mind giving your opinion, then maybe you won't mind telling me what you think about the seafood restaurant near your store?"

There was no way he knew I hated that place. Why did his eyes twinkle like he knew something?

"Come on," he said. "You can tell – oh, hello." He reached down to pet Sunshine who was swishing herself around my ankles. "A cat." He said to me, confused.

"Yes," I replied simply.

"Do you think he's lost?" He was snapping his fingers and leaning down to try to get Sunshine's attention. "That's a pretty solid harness. Someone must be nearby, looking for him."

Sunshine looked up at me and jumped into my arms when I slightly patted my chest in a signal she knew well. "She isn't lost," I said, reaching around to my side backpack pocket to grab the leash that snapped easily into her harness.

I knew it was weird that I took my cat with me to the woods. If it would have been a dog, I suppose it would have been cool, but because Sunshine was a cat, it was just weird. And maybe pathetic. But she loved being outside, and I loved having her with me. I had some striking shots of her from these treks. She was really good about following the trails with me – often in trees. She came when I called, and she was fine on the leash when she knew it was time. She understood the drill if she wanted to come.

Anthony looked at me and Sunshine, a smile on his face. "Well, that's a surprise."

"Okay, so we need to get back now." I stepped by him quickly and began marching along the trail as fast as I could. "It was good to see you," I said over my shoulder. *Good to see you?* Had I lost my mind? It most certainly was not good to see him.

"Sure. Good to see you too," he called as I booked it along the trail.

Chapter 3

"I'm still worried about the benefits line," Ruthie said as she and I sat in the small café area of the Co-op going over the financial reports. "I know we want to be generous, but that number is high. I really think staff should be kicking in more for their health insurance."

This was hard for me. Ruthie was amazing. I even thought of her as a mentor. She was a retired doctor's wife. She'd worked for various charities over the years and had been the Co-op's board president for as long as I'd worked there. She had taught me how to do the books and reports, so I could take on new responsibilities and work my way into my current role. She was really a force of goodness. She was kind, compassionate, caring, and gave of her free time for deserving causes. But she was *so* out of touch. I didn't feel the same impatience with her that I often felt around people who had lots of money and resources. I knew she was a good person. But I didn't know what to say when she started on things like this. She talked a lot about the Co-op being a good employer and making sure the organization took care of its employees – both in compensation and working conditions. But when she said stuff like this…

I could tell her that if I didn't have another income source, I, as the highest paid staffer, would have a hard time paying more for my health insurance. Or I could try to get there another way without having to expose myself – at talking about my other source of income and about the vulnerability I felt at being… not like her. At not having money. At being less than her.

Ugh. I hated this.

"I get what you're saying, Ruthie. I just have some concern about increasing the employee portion – especially for the new employees who are on the lower end of the pay scale. The insurance has pretty high co-pays anyway, so I'm afraid people will not really be able to go to the doctor and probably will just not take the insurance even if they need it."

Ruthie looked conflicted. She was compassionate, but she was also a shrewd businesswoman. She didn't only see the numbers on the balance sheet – it was like she actually felt them. "Have you heard of that happening?" she asked. "Employees not going to the doctor?"

"I think so," I hedged. I knew I certainly questioned how important it was for me to go because of the expense. It was hard to explain to someone like Ruthie that these were regular people problems when it was such a given for regular people.

"Well, we don't want that," she said. "We'll need to keep an eye on it. Maybe I'll reach out to someone from the hospital charity ball committee to see if they have any recommendations about ways to get our premiums down."

Relieved that we had averted a hard look at getting employees to contribute more, I said, "That sounds great. Thanks, Ruthie."

"Other than that concern, the reports are in good shape. The prepared product line is doing really well. The bottom line here should make the board members feel comfortable with the increased expense we took on with the slight wage increases."

She tucked the reports into a folder and said, "Okay, now how are *you* doing? Did you have a good weekend?"

"Yes, I did. I went to my parents and then I got some hiking in."

"No work crises?"

"Well, I took a few calls. Sorted out a few things for Brendan."

"And your parents? How much did you need to do there?"

"Nothing at all," I said honestly. Ruthie didn't know the extent of it, but she knew that my parents were a time pressure that I sometimes had to balance with my work.

I'd been about eighteen when I'd understood our farm was in trouble financially. I'd been about eighteen and a half when I'd understood why. My father was a hard-working farmer. He could repair old tractors, sometimes even build a new part. He could work all day and go at it hard again the next day. But what he couldn't do was keep the books, make projections, build efficiencies. He had buried us so deeply – refinancing the farm over and over during the housing boom. The banks kept telling him the property was increasing in value, and he kept borrowing more and more money against it to keep things afloat. By the time the housing bust happened, the farm was so far underwater, the end was inevitable. We had fought as hard as we could. I'd dropped any dreams about leaving home or attending college. I had started working full-time and took over the household finances. I helped my dad in any free time I had. We poured everything we had into trying to save the farm, but ultimately, the bank won.

The foreclosure had been humiliating. The word itself – foreclosure – was the most vile word I'd ever heard. Everyone knew what had been happening. Max Parker had tried to keep things quiet when he'd made an offer to the bank to buy our farm while they were basically evicting us. He'd even tried to convince the bank to give my dad some of the proceeds if he offered more than the bank was asking, and he'd tried to make it seem like a regular sale to anyone paying attention, but the gossips like Tammy Larkins at the bank spread the word. Everyone knew.

Ruthie knew, but I don't think she knew how much it bothered me. I tried hard to keep that part to myself. She also knew that my parents leaned on me. Again, she didn't know the extent of it all – just that it sometimes was a tension for me.

Sensing my thoughts were affecting my demeanor, I tried to cheer things up by reinforcing that my parents hadn't needed me at all over the weekend. "They had me over to give me a birthday dinner. It was great," I added with a smile I hoped was convincing.

"Your birthday? In all these years, I've never known when your birthday was. Happy birthday!" Ruthie stood to her full height, which only brought her a few inches over my head while I was still seated. She reached down to hug me to her. "This is perfect," she continued. "It will line up perfectly with what I was going to ask you."

"Ask me?" I started gathering up the papers spread out on the table.

"Yes! I have a favor to ask. But this way, I can thank you for it with a little birthday celebration. I wanted to see if you would come to my house to share some of your expertise for the benefit of one of my charities. Now you can come, and I'll do a birthday lunch!"

Ruthie beamed, and I panicked a little. I'd never been to Ruthie's house. I'd never met her husband, Dr. Marsh. I'd heard her talk about Loren Marsh over the years, but, as much as I liked and respected Ruthie, I'd been able to keep our relationship confined to the Co-op and the occasional downtown bite to eat when she insisted on taking me to lunch or coffee.

I didn't want to socialize with Ruthie and her husband. And deal with one of her charities. As much as Ruthie was a part of the community and as much as I liked and respected her, I didn't belong in her world. Even talking about "charities" the way she did… It made my stomach turn.

"Oh, no need for that at all, Ruthie," I said, really hoping I could get out of this. "My birthday has come and gone. And you know I'm happy to answer any questions you have now if I can help you with something."

"No, no. I insist," she said puffing out her little chest, indicating her answer was firm. "I need you to meet with someone who's trying to brainstorm ideas to help Spruce Lake out of some struggles they're having."

"Spruce Lake… the music camp?" I asked, confused.

"Yes, but the answer might be related to a food venture. That's why I need you. I've already tried to answer as much as I can, but I really need your first-hand knowledge for this. Besides, Loren is annoyed that he's never gotten to meet you. Come this Saturday for lunch." Her tone was firm. She had this quality that I found fascinating. She could be so compassionate and caring, but when she meant business, it was very clear. She scared most people when she was in this mode.

"What about Saturday afternoon?" I asked. "Maybe just afternoon coffee or something like that? I don't want you to go to any trouble and – "

"It's no trouble! What are you going on about? I want to do it! And I do need your help."

"But isn't Saturday Shabbat for you?"

"We're observing Friday night, but we're looser on Saturday. Come at one o'clock. You know where I live."

Oh, yeah, did I ever know where she lived. Right along the shoreline where some of the nicest houses in the area were.

I sighed and nodded my head. "What can I bring?" I asked, defeated.

"Nothing, you silly girl! Yourself – and your knowledge. That's all I want." She patted my shoulder as she secured her bag firmly on her shoulder and turned to go.

∞ ∞ ∞

Later that day, I slipped out of the store for what I hoped would be a restorative break. Brendan was struggling as a manager. He loved to have a good time and, while I was happy to see our staff having fun at work, he didn't have the ability to shift into work mode when he needed to. Everyone loved him – customers and co-workers – but no one was actually getting much work done while he was managing a shift. I was going to have to deal with it soon, but, in the meantime, I was killing myself even more than usual trying to keep up with my responsibilities and cover for all the work that wasn't happening on the floor.

I just need fifteen minutes, I told myself as I gripped my coffee and headed toward a bench in a nearby park that overlooked one of our lakes.

I settled onto the bench and let my gaze rest on various points, taking mental pictures. Imagining how it would look captured with my camera. I let my mind become lost in the exercise, so I could mentally escape for a few minutes.

"So, is there a cat around that I should be aware of?" The voice snapped me out of my happy place, and I looked up to see Anthony Kaplan's tall figure backlit by the sun. I couldn't see his expression, but I could hear a little amused smirk in his voice. I'm sure having a cat on a hike with me contributed to his picture of me as a small-town simpleton.

"No cat today," I said, beginning to stand. "Here." I gestured to the bench. "I was just leaving."

"It didn't look that way," Anthony said. "You looked pretty invested in the view. How about if we share the bench for a few minutes?" He'd moved out of the sun, so I could see his face clearly now. He was smiling as usual. He really belonged in a toothpaste ad. Or any kind of beautiful man ad – skin care, hair care, eyeglasses. He would look really great in glasses with his piercing blue eyes.

Realizing I was staring, I shifted and sank back down on the bench. I looked out at the lake and tried to ignore that this random tourist unsettled me so much. He sat on the bench as well, leaving a few feet between us. I braced myself, expecting him to begin asking more questions or making comments on my store, my town, my cat, myself.

But he just... didn't. He sat on the bench and was quiet. It was awkward. But *he* didn't seem awkward. The energy coming from his side of the bench was ease and comfort. While I knew my energy was chaos and curiosity. *What the hell was he doing? Why did he keep trying to interact with me when I was doing my best to brush him off? Again, where the hell were his people and what the hell was he doing here – asking about food wholesale opportunities and which hiking trails were the best? When would he just go away?*

I spent the next five minutes in tense anxiety instead of the relaxing calm I'd hoped for. Anthony didn't say anything. He just looked at the lake and watched birds and gave a little laugh when a squirrel lost its balance as it scampered along a fallen branch near the shoreline. Anthony stretched his long legs in front of him and crossed his ankles. I took in his slim khaki pants hugging his thighs and casual gray sneakers. I glanced at my own skinny jeans and Birks, feeling underdressed. But, underdressed for what, I didn't know. *For sitting beside him?* Maybe. My mom's constant criticism of my appearance was ringing in my ears.

A little confused by sharing the silence, I finished off my coffee and stood to go. "So, I'm headed back to work now. I'll see you around," I said, hoping I was wrong about seeing him at all.

"I'm headed that way, too. I'll walk you back."

I huffed in frustration. I didn't understand what was going on. Why didn't he have better things to do with his time? He was clearly a successful person in whatever it was he did in life. He walked and talked with an air of confidence that was commanding. He was absolutely accustomed to getting anything he wanted.

"Is my company that disagreeable?" he asked, falling

into step next to me. I sped up, now wanting to get back to work as soon as I could.

"I just have a lot to do," I said, noticing Chris walking out of the hardware store a little ahead of us.

"Busy day for cashiers?" he asked.

I looked at his smiling, friendly face and wanted to spit in it. "I'm sure it's not what you're used to, but, yes, we are busy at the store."

I practically ran to catch up to Chris to get away from this condescending man. It was the worst kind of condescension. The kind that happens when someone is actually kind of nice, and they don't even understand they are being insulting. Ruthie had an element of it, but I forgave it, overlooked it – because she was so dear and had the best of intentions. This clueless, privileged man – not the same. At all.

"Chris!" I shouted. Anthony's long legs kept up with my half jog up the street. Chris looked up, surprised but happy to see me. He didn't look quite as happy when he saw Anthony as well.

"Hey, Willow." He reached for the side of my waist and brought me in to give me a kiss on the cheek.

"How are you?" His eyes scanned my face. I could only imagine what my face was saying. Probably something like, "Help me!"

Chris let me go a bit and turned to Anthony, "Hey, man."

"Chris, how are you doing?" Anthony greeted.

They exchanged a very firm handshake. "You're still in town," Chris said with a hint of a question in his tone.

"Oh, I'm here for a while," Anthony said. "I'm not passing through."

What? My brain stuttered. *He wasn't leaving?*

I missed the next exchange between them while overcoming my surprise at this news. I realized Chris had pulled me into his side and was talking to me about weekend plans.

"And I thought we might fit in some kayaking before it gets too cold." Chris looked at me expectantly. I looked at Anthony and his smile was different but still present.

"Sorry. This weekend? Is that what you were asking?"

"Yeah, Willow," Chris said with a touch of impatience. He glanced uncomfortably at Anthony. "I was saying it would be great to take you out in the kayaks like I've been telling you about. Maybe Saturday?" he asked hopefully.

"Oh, sorry, Chris, I can't," I responded, uncomfortably. "I have a thing on Saturday. It's work. Sort of."

"I thought you weren't working on weekends anymore," Chris said.

We made a really odd trio on the street. Chris was trying to move things forward with me, Anthony was strangely hanging around, and I just wanted to just get away from both men. Like some mixed up magnet ends attracting and repelling each other.

Before I could get a response out, Anthony said, "Weekends must be a really busy time in the store. I'm sure Willow must not have a lot of control over that."

"I'm sorry," Chris said, letting the irritation show in the tone of his voice. "I'm not sure what you think you know about Willow's work, but maybe you could give us just a minute here." He gripped my elbow and began shifting us away from where Anthony was standing.

"Of course," Anthony said but just turned to look into the hardware storefront instead of walking away.

"So, what do you think about this weekend?" Chris asked me. "The weather is supposed to be great. We could head out early and make a day of it. What do you say?"

I did not think spending a day with Chris was a good idea until I had a chance to make sure we were on the same page about our dating status. Until I was sure he was clear that I wasn't looking for anything more than casual.

"Sorry, Chris, I've really got to do something for work. It's a board member asking, so I can't really say no."

Chris pulled me a little closer to him and asked quietly, "When are we going to find some time together, huh? I'm tied up on Sunday. I really want to do something soon."

A few doors down, I saw the Co-op door open, and Brendan looked desperately up and down the street until his eyes locked on me. "Willow!" he shouted. "I think we need some help."

"I'll text you," I said quickly extricating myself from Chris's grasp and jogging toward the Co-op. I looked back as I stepped inside and saw Chris and Anthony still rooted in place.

∞∞∞

"Thank God," Brendan said as I stepped inside.

I looked up and couldn't believe how bad things had gotten in the twenty minutes I'd been gone. Things really shouldn't be this hard. The closing shift was supposed to make sure the store was stocked for the next day. Throughout the day, I usually had one person working the floor, two cashiers, and one to two floaters who did whatever was needed. When I wasn't around or when I was busy with the things I was actually supposed to spend my time on – the business side of things – I also had a shift manager working. Brendan was that shift manager today, and he'd somehow let the easy flow of things turn into complete chaos.

Despite starting off stocked first thing that morning, there were obvious gaps and holes where items had not been replaced throughout the day. And I knew we weren't out of stock. The floor person just wasn't doing her job. The obvious crush she had on Brendan gave me some idea about what had distracted her.

She was surrounded by a couple of customers who were asking whether we had a few things in the back. There were lines at the cash registers much deeper than they should have been, and even regular customers in those lines were showing irritation. And the disaster that prompted Brendan to come find me... Someone had broken a glass bottle of milk. It had spilled both in the cooler and all over the floor and there was broken glass everywhere.

I honestly couldn't believe things had fallen apart so quickly. I told Brendan to go stand in front of the broken glass and not move until I could get over to help him. Then I raced over to Mindy who had the line of customers looking for missing items from the shelves. I immediately assessed it could be solved by giving her specific instructions to begin with their items (which were all fresh produce) and then replenish all the produce items before continuing with baked goods and then the regular shelves. Next on the list was checking on my cashiers to understand why things were so backed up. As was often the case, all the glitches were happening at once – one cashier was out of single dollar bills so couldn't make change for someone, the other had receipt tape that had ended and the spare rolls weren't under her register where they should have been. And Brendan had been MIA when they needed him to solve these simple problems.

I worked my way through one issue after another – getting coffee started for the self-serve thermoses where there were some annoyed customers hanging around near the empty ones and finally getting the mop bucket, broom, and cleaning cart out to the milk mess where Brendan stood. As I started the cleanup and tried to be as directive as I could with Brendan about his next steps to keep things running, he decided it was a good time to tell me that the bathroom toilet was clogged… again.

It was later than usual that night when I finally locked the store. I knew I was going to have to do something about Brendan. It was a current theme in my life. At work, I needed to do something about Brendan. In my personal life, I needed to do something about

Chris. As much as I loved the Co-op and recognized that my long history with it now made it part of my identity, I was so very tired.

Although it was clear Anthony Kaplan looked down on me because I was "just a cashier," I began sort of wishing he was right. Doing everyone else's job during the day and trying to fit my own in at the end of the day and on weekends was wearing me down.

Chapter 4

Saturday morning, I was close to deciding what I would wear to Ruthie's for lunch when my phone rang.

"Critter, I think we could use your help," my dad's anguished voice came across the line.

Not my favorite way to start a weekend, but I couldn't say it was completely unusual. Feeling almost like it was a lucky distraction from my dread about lunch at Ruthie's, I pulled on the navy dress I'd selected. It was long-sleeved but the fabric was light enough for the September day. I paired it with a belt, tights, and my well-loved, brown leather boots. I quickly worked my long hair into a braid across my left shoulder and had to believe it was enough for a visit to Ruthie's house.

"Hey, Dad," I said as I was getting out of my car. He'd come out to greet me in the driveway, which was an indication of how bad it was.

"Critter," he said in his attempt at a whisper. His gruff voice made it hard. "She's woken half the neighborhood. It started last night, but she finally fell asleep for a few hours. Then she started up again early this morning and hasn't stopped.

"Your uncle Mark came over last night. He made some comment about her not getting any younger. Hell, he was talking about all of us. That none of us are getting any younger. But you know your mom. She heard something different, and now she just can't stop."

My dad was glancing around nervously at the nearby houses. Growing up on the farm, my mom's episodes were less of an issue – at least in this respect. She could be as loud as she wanted to be most of the time, and the only people who had to listen to it were my dad and me. But, moving into this little house with neighbors a few feet away was tough. For a woman who primarily cared what other people thought of her, she could quickly forget that in the middle of an episode.

"Okay," I said, patting his arm. "Let's go inside."

"Mom?" I asked as we opened the door.

"You fuckin' bastard!" she snarled at my dad. "Of course, you had to call your 'precious critter' to come see." She sat near a window that looked out into the small back yard. She looked ten years older than she normally looked. Her face was drawn, and she was wearing one of my dad's old flannel shirts over loose pants. Her hair was badly in need of brushing. But mostly it was the scowl. The scowl that highlighted the small lines around her eyes and mouth. It turned her beautiful face into a scary, ugly sight.

"And you," she said, sizing me up. "Get the hell out of my house, you trumped-up dyke."

Well, that was a new one. I had thought she was out of new insults for me, but clearly, I'd been wrong.

"Mom, you need to calm down and tell me what's going on."

"What's going on? I'll tell you what's going on, *Critter*," she uttered my dad's nickname for me with venom spilling from her tongue. "Your dad's stupid brother thinks he can come into *my* house and insult *me*. And your simpering, weak-willed father thinks it's okay. He *agrees* with him. Calling *me* old. With their haggard faces and pot bellies. Especially, Mark, eating at truck stops all the time. He couldn't even keep his wife. She was smart to leave his sorry ass years ago. And *he's* going to call *me* old."

"Mom, are you sure that's what he said? Uncle Mark thinks you're great." I might have been stretching that truth a bit. "I don't really think that's what he said. I know he doesn't think that." My uncle Mark knew better. He actually should have known better than to even mention his own age because that was enough to set her off. Anything was really enough to set her off. It was a minefield.

"He did say that," she shouted at the top of her lungs. The shout lingered in the air, reverberating off the walls in the small room. I didn't respond. I just waited because I could see what was coming.

Her scowl morphed into a childish pout, and she began to cry. Through the tears and the sobbing, she said, "I am old. I'm washed up and useless." She beat her hands against her chest as she continued saying things about how she was "worthless." How she was "over the hill" and "pathetic" and how we would all be "better off without her."

The "better off without her" was a common refrain. The parts about her age had increased over the last few years, but it had always been something, even when I was growing up, and she still had her youth. The "better off without her" and being "worthless" was what it usually boiled down to though.

"Mom, come on. You know we don't think that."

"Yes, you do!" Her scowl returned as she directed her shout to me. "You think you're better than all of us. You're really just a slut. Can't settle down with one man. Can't even try. Because you think you're too good."

"Too good for what, Mom?" I pushed down any of my own emotion before it could swell. It never mattered whether she hurt my feelings or not, so I'd learned years before to try not to react. "You're not being fair. I don't think I'm better than anyone." I wanted to tell her she was being ridiculous. I wanted to shout back at her. Sometimes I still lost my temper and did, but most of the time, I knew it slowed down the process. That I had to go through the steps with her and let her say the awful things she was going to say. I let her words scramble in my mind as she continued – tried to not actually hear the things she was saying at this point.

"Come on," I coaxed when she took a break. "You know Uncle Mark didn't mean anything. He thinks you're beautiful. Everyone thinks so. And, of course, we're not better off without you. Why would we still be here if we felt that way?"

"Your dad would be better off. He deserves someone better than me." The frenzied energy in her was starting to fade. She was moving into the pitiful stage of the process.

"That's not true, honey," my dad said, bring a fresh cup of coffee to her. "Here, honey. I just made it."

"Mom," I said, as my dad set the cup of coffee down next to her. "If dad didn't adore you, he wouldn't be here. We love you."

"I should just end it all," she whispered. "Your lives would be easier without me. You're both a couple of martyrs." With each statement, she increased her volume. "You don't really love me; you just keep doing your good deed. Taking care of the freak." She beat her fist against her chest again as she said "freak."

"Mom, stop. You're not a freak. Please, stop. We love you so much."

This back and forth continued for another hour or more. When my mom's episode settled into anguish and regret, she and I found ourselves on the back steps with more coffee. She was quietly crying at this point with a pile of tissues in her lap. My dad was inside waiting for the storm to completely clear.

"How are you so patient, Willow? I don't understand." Her lip began to quiver, and she let out a low moan as she cried some more.

"But I'm sorry," she said, wiping her nose with the crumpled tissue. "I know you shouldn't have to take care of me." She trailed off and wiped her eyes. "I just hate that Mark though. He *does* think he's some kind of catch and he's just –"

"Mom," I said in a warning voice. "Enough. You know Uncle Mark is sweet. Just like dad."

"He's *not* like your father," she said. Then in a loving voice, she said, "No one is like your father."

"Okay. I'll give you that." I put my arm around her shoulder and leaned my head against hers. "Okay now?"

I asked.

"I'm fine. I'm sorry, honey."

"It's okay, Mom. We just worry about you. You have to stop thinking those things about yourself. You know that's not what we think of you. You're telling yourself that – it's not coming from us."

"Okay, okay. I'll try." She looked at me. She really took me in for the first time since I'd arrived. "Well, don't you look nice? I've never seen you wear that dress."

"Thanks, Mom."

"Now, if you would just put on some makeup and do something with your hair, you would look just lovely."

∞∞∞

By the time I arrived at Ruthie's house, I was depleted. I didn't even have the energy to be nervous anymore. I just wanted to sleep the rest of the weekend and cuddle with Sunshine.

Ruthie's house sat proudly along the biggest lake in our area. It was a subtle blue with white trim and had an impressive circular driveway, which I now found myself sitting in. The entrance had glass on the front and the back so you could see straight across a large entry way to the lake on the back side of the house.

Ruthie opened the door as I was getting out of my car and greeted me excitedly. "I'm so glad you made it! I've wanted to have you over forever." She gave me a big hug, and I tried to muster some enthusiasm. I handed her a bouquet of flowers I had picked up on my way. "Is this okay?" I asked. I'd googled a little about Shabbat before I came and had seen that sometimes people observing it couldn't even accept a gift while it was happening.

"Totally fine. And so lovely!" she said, taking the flowers from me.

She led me into the house where I was met with an imposing older man who had something close to a handlebar mustache. He could only be Dr. Loren Marsh.

"And you must be the famous Willow! Aren't you a picture?" he said, stepping toward me to give me a hug. "It's about time. Ruthie goes on and on about you. I can't believe we haven't met before now."

"Nice to meet you, Dr. Marsh. I could say the same. I hear all about you as well from Ruthie." *And I would be a picture if I'd put on makeup and fixed my hair*, I heard my mother's voice say.

I was led through the room of glass into a large area with vaulted ceilings that had a kitchen on the driveway side of the house and a living area on the lake side of the house. The living area had rich brocade, overstuffed furniture facing a wall of windows overlooking the lake. The style was a little formal for a lake house, but Ruthie had chosen a cream and light pink pattern that softened some of the heaviness. As I made my way fully into the living area, I nearly tripped over my feet when I realized that Anthony Kaplan sat in one of the chairs flanking the couch. He looked as surprised to see me as I was to see him.

"Willow?" he asked standing and looking to Ruthie. "Aunt Ruth?" he asked.

Aunt Ruth? Was this really happening?

"You've met?" Ruthie asked, looking between us.

"Yes," I said. "We have."

Anthony jumped in. "Aunt Ruth, you know I've been to the Co-op several times. I told you I'd met some people there and tried to talk to the Operations Director you mentioned." He turned to me and said, "Are you joining the director today?" His usual smile was absent, and he seemed a little annoyed.

"Anthony," Ruthie said in a scolding tone. "Willow *is* the director I mentioned."

"I'm sorry. What?" he asked in disbelief.

"And Anthony is your... nephew." I stated, putting together lots of puzzle pieces.

"But you're the cashier," he said.

I looked at Ruthie who was giving her nephew a stern look. I felt bad for her. Like I said, Ruthie had her less sensitive moments, but her heart was *always* in the right place. And she was sensitive enough to know that Anthony was being transparent in his condescension.

I loved Ruthie too much to let this be uncomfortable for her. "Well, it's nice to meet you more formally, Anthony. I guess we're both here to help Ruthie."

Anthony shook his head a few times as if physically shaking off his surprise.

"Let's go to the dining room." Ruthie began to lead the way through an opening on the other side of the living area. "I have roast and a potato kugel."

Mr. Eager had left town. The man who sat with me at Ruthie's heavy dining room table was no longer the smiling, easygoing man I'd been bumping into. He was a disapproving, suspicious, silent onlooker.

Ruthie was running the show, and, so far, the show had been small talk. Shop talk about the Co-op. With some stories thrown in for Dr. Marsh's benefit. The experience was still somewhat intimidating, but despite the fancy meal (none of my mother's nine by thirteen pans hitting this table), the light classical music playing in the background, and the perfect manners of everyone at the table, Ruthie and Dr. Marsh were genuine and kind. Ruthie in her expensive home was the same Ruthie I saw in my cramped office at work.

"This girl," she said to her husband. "Well, you know, we just wouldn't be able to function without her. I saw her using her problem-solving skills when she was barely out of high school working as a cashier and stocker. She's mastered all of it. Does the work of five people."

"Ruthie, honestly, this is too much." I tried to laugh off the praise. It would have been sweet because I knew she really meant it, but it was embarrassing in front of someone like Anthony. I still didn't know what he did for a living, but even though he now knew I wasn't "just a cashier" (as if there was anything wrong with that), I knew my actual role still fell short of anything that would fall on his scale of impressiveness.

"No, no, no!" her voice pitched up with each word as she punctuated each one with pats on the table. "It's all true. The only thing we have to work on is the management piece."

Well, this was embarrassing. I guess in addition to praising me in front of her husband and nephew, she also thought it was time for my evaluation.

"I've finally gotten her to slow down on the weekends," she continued, looking from Anthony to Dr. Marsh. "But she has some problem people working at the store, and they need to be disciplined or let go." She turned to me. "You need people you can trust, Willow. Like I said, you're doing the work of five people, but I only want you doing the work of three." She smiled at me. "To be able to strike some work/life balance."

"She's right, Willow," Dr. Marsh looked at his wife

affectionately. It was easy to see the older couple still adored each other. "But don't let her fool you. I've seen her struggle with the same thing – many times. It comes from caring too much, which can never be a bad thing."

Ruthie began to interrupt her husband, but he stopped her, putting his hand over hers. "Now, Ruth, you know it's true. Do you remember that secretary you wouldn't fire at the women's shelter? She'd been a resident there, and you gave her a shot at the job, but she just wasn't doing the work. You worked for hours every day after she left to finish what she should have done."

Ruthie let out an exasperated breath. "Yes, but I'm trying to help Willow learn from my experience." She looked at me and smiled. "I just don't want you to burn out. I want you to take care of yourself. It's important to me." Her words were heartfelt and kind.

It should have been a lovely moment. I felt my eyes start to water and considered getting up to give her a hug. But the moment was completely eclipsed by Anthony who stood and said, "Right. Are we heading back into the living room for coffee?" He dropped his linen napkin on the table and turned on his heel.

We finished the birthday festivities of the day in the living room after Ruthie served us all a beautiful blueberry vegan cake she'd special ordered from Lanie Parker. I knew a little about Ruthie's mostly Kosher diet because it influenced some of what we kept on the shelves in the Co-op. So, while it was unusual for most people to have a roast dinner followed by a vegan cake, I knew it had something to do with the Kosher rules.

After I put my cake plate down on the coffee table in front of me, Ruthie said it was time for the business portion of the afternoon. Anthony, who had refused any of my birthday cake, huffed impatiently as if to say, "Finally."

"Willow, you know I'm on the board at Spruce Lake Music Camp." She looked at me, and I nodded. "Well, they're in a bit of trouble. They still attract the best classical music teachers and are able to charge top tier tuition because of that, but there's more competition now than there used to be. Teachers and students have more choices, so as costs increase, we can't just keep raising the tuition. The competition has created a bit of a ceiling and we're there." She looked over at Anthony who had stood up. He now had his back to us and was looking through the wall of windows out to the lake.

"Also," Ruthie continued, "and, most pressingly, there are some facilities issues that are going to have to be dealt with over the next few years. There are some things that need attention now, and it will become a crisis if some of the bigger items aren't dealt with soon. We're applying for some grants, but it would be better to find a longer-term, self-sustaining solution."

I was confused. I still couldn't understand what I was doing here. I knew absolutely nothing about music or camps or facilities. I looked at Ruthie blankly.

"Anthony's father - my brother - founded Kaplan Construction, which is a well-known commercial construction and development company. Anthony has been running things for the last ten years, but recently decided to sell. With Anthony at the helm, the company mostly specialized in hotel development. I've recruited him to help us find some solutions at Spruce Lake – both with business ventures as well as the facilities issues."

Of course, he was the head of a company like that. Silver-spooned Richie Rich who could sell up and do charity work when he wanted to. What in the world had I been sucked into? I did not belong here.

"That's great," I said, still confused. "Sounds like the perfect fit."

"Yes, it is. Anthony's got some great ideas. And some great connections. But they aren't local connections. That's where you come in. A lot of the ideas involve local food, and you are the person who is connected with everyone in that area."

Anthony was still standing with his back to me, hand in his pocket, pretty as you please.

"Ruthie, I can give you a vendor list. That will give you everything you need. If you'd explained before, I could have brought it with me. Or just given it to you… or you," I said, turning my head in Anthony's direction. "It's not a secret who the area farmers and food producers are."

"Exactly," Anthony said. He turned my direction but didn't look at me. "Aunt Ruth, I told you this. I can work through a list easily and get us what we need. Hell, I don't even need you to make a list. It would have been nice, but I can get what I need from the signs in the store." His piercing blue eyes were icy, and he turned to me and said, "I think we've actually got this. It's become overcomplicated, and it didn't need to be."

This. This is what I'd been waiting for from this man. This was him living up to my expectations. I had even started feeling guilty that I kept expecting him to be an entitled jerk because mostly he'd been nice. Aside from him looking down on me. There was that. But, otherwise, he'd always been friendly. Almost kind. This side of him - this is what I'd been waiting for.

"Okay, then," I said, standing up. "Ruthie, thank you so much for having me over. Lunch was beautiful and it was so nice to finally meet Dr. Marsh. Please thank him as well." I was making my way across the room, trying to get out of there as soon as I could.

"Now, wait just a minute, young lady." Ruthie used all the force her seventy-year-old frame had to grip my arm and guide me back to my seat. "I'm not finished."

I sat back in the chair. Anthony looked at Ruthie, expectantly.

She turned her intense gaze to him. I hadn't really noticed any resemblance before, but they both had this ability to be agreeable and charming and then suddenly become serious and fierce. I suspected they had different motivations for their transformations, but they were similar in their ability. "Anthony Michael," she said sternly. "Sit down and stop being rude to my guest. To my friend."

Anthony glanced between the two of us and ducked his head a bit, making his way to a chair.

"Look," he said. "I'm not trying to be rude." He rearranged the coffee cup and creamer dish in front of him on the table. He looked at me and said, "I'm sorry." Then he looked to Ruthie and said, "Sincerely, I apologize. It's just… This is business. This is what I do. I'm just trying to be efficient here."

"This is *not* business," Ruthie said. "This is the arts fabric of our region. Of our state. This is preserving a local treasure. That's what this is."

I felt so out of place. Anthony was the jerk I expected him to be, but I had to admit he wasn't wrong. There was no reason I was here. I didn't understand what Ruthie thought she was doing. I had no business discussing "the arts fabric of our state."

"Here's my proposal," she said, beginning to take the dishes Anthony had been fiddling with out of his hands and stacking them neatly in front of her. "This Wednesday evening, I would like both of you to meet with the director of Spruce Lake. She will show you around the grounds, and I'd like everyone to brainstorm some ideas together." She turned more fully to me. "Willow, most of the ideas really do have a local food element. I value your knowledge and your judgement. I'd really appreciate if you would be there."

"Ruthie, thank you. Really. That means a lot. I'm more than happy to prepare some materials for you to take to that meeting. I think –" Jeez, this hurt to even say out loud. "I think Anthony is right. It would be better for you all to take it from there if I can just provide some written information."

Ruthie started talking again as if I hadn't said a word. "I value your expertise so much, Willow, that I won't allow you to help without compensating you. I know how busy you are with the store, your parents, that... What's his name this time? Chris?"

Wow, she made it sound like I cycled through men.

"You're very busy. And while I can't ask the camp to compensate you, given their circumstances, I can certainly do it, and I'd be happy to." She looked at me and waited.

That cunning little wizard. I had been one hundred percent determined to get myself out of this, and she knew it, which is why she pulled out this magic piece of manipulation. I couldn't allow her to pay me for a favor, but the fact that she was offering to pay me made it impossible for me to refuse to "help out." I'd been manipulated by her before at the Co-op. It always came from a good place, but it never felt good to be manipulated. She would do whatever it took to whomever though, as a means to an end that she thought was worthwhile.

"Ruthie, I'm not taking money from you," I said, defeated. "I'll do the thing on Wednesday. Where should I go?"

"That's wonderful!" Ruthie had the nerve to act surprised when she knew exactly what she'd been doing. "We're going to meet right at Spruce Lake. Emerson is the director, and she's already on board.

Have you been there before?"

Had I been there before? Of course, I hadn't been there before. I mean, I had been to the lake but not the camp for rich kids studying classical music. "No," I said simply.

"Look for the signs to the dining hall when you get there. That's where we'll meet."

I stood to leave again, and, this time, Ruthie and Anthony also stood, indicating I was free to go.

"Aunt Ruth, is that photo from the same artist who has work for sale at the Co-op?" Anthony asked, looking past my shoulder to the wall behind me.

She nodded that it was.

"I thought so. I was admiring it the last time I visited. I've noticed them the last few times I was at the store. What a place for art like that. Some people just don't know what they've got."

And on that note, I really did take my leave.

Chapter 5

The next day, I was longing to get outside for another hike, but things had been so busy lately and I was behind on orders. The photo Anthony asked about? Yeah, that was mine.

My side hustle was my favorite thing to do, but it also took precious time that I didn't have. This was one of those days when I had to forgo my desire to get outside and actually take some pictures to instead make sure I replenished some of my stock at a few galleries that sold my work.

Of course, I had conflicting emotions when Anthony unknowingly complimented me while at the same time, intentionally insulted me. I did pretty well with my side business. I hung photos at the Co-op in the café area, and they were purchased frequently enough.

Recently, there had been a slight uptick even. I hoped the uptick wasn't going to draw more of Ruthie's attention on the financials. For now, I was mixed in with a line item for miscellaneous vendor payments, and Ruthie had been okay with it when I told her this vendor preferred to stay anonymous and to be paid in cash. I did have to issue a tax document to myself, so if she really looked, she would know it was me. But, so far, I'd been able to keep my secret safe.

The gallery owners knew who I was, of course, but I didn't work with anyone who was closer than fifty miles from my little town. I had a little bit of a name among that group as a local art photographer. But I didn't have a website or do any advertising. It wasn't like I was running any risk of being found out by people I knew.

Any why did I want to keep it a secret from them? It just felt so vulnerable. And private. I knew someone like Ruthie would probably be very encouraging, but I knew people in my life like my mom would tell me I was doing something uppity and tell me I was being ridiculous. I was okay with keeping it to myself. It fed my creative side, and it gave me the extra money I needed to slip monthly payments into my parents' account to cover their mortgage and some extras.

Since I'd taken over the books and helped my parents get into the small house they now lived in, I had been supplementing their income. My dad trusted me to take care of the finances. He also felt mountains of shame about losing the farm and managing that aspect of it poorly, so it was a sensitive topic, and we mostly just avoided it. After my mom's most recent episode, I resolved to increase my monthly contribution a little bit, and I planned to tell them they had a little more money in their monthly disposable income allowance. Oh, how my mother hated that – I recommended an amount that they could spend each month on extras and when she was feeling snarky, she called it her *allowance*.

Today would be spent in my second bedroom, which I had converted into my studio. As frugal as my past had taught me to be, this room was where I spent my money. I had the best computer, monitor, and large format printer I felt I could afford, along with multi drawer roller carts for organizing and storing my prints. Sunshine would also rather be outside on a day like today, but I had window hammocks, cozy baskets, and a cat tree for her. She made herself comfortable when she knew it was one of those days.

 I sat at my desk editing some of the photos I'd taken the day I'd run into Anthony in the woods. I edited the picture of the beaver working on his dam, but I saw Anthony's yellow running shoes, beating a path through the woods. I pulled up some other shots of Sunshine resting on a limb in the tree, but what I saw was Anthony's perfect smile as he looked up at me in surprise after seeing Sunshine in the woods.

 Grrr. This man was beyond frustrating. He had finally met my negative expectations, and somehow my primitive hormones still reacted to him.

 If he didn't have such a low opinion of me, he would actually be the perfect candidate for my ideal no strings, no future relationship. At least, my eyes and my body certainly thought so, but my mind told me he wouldn't feel the same. He could look anywhere for the casual date and definitely wouldn't be looking my way. And I wouldn't be able to tolerate his smug privilege.

I sighed and hit the print button, watching two copies of the beaver picture appear from the large format printer. I also printed two copies of five of my best sellers, ready to sign them all. I signed the ones for sale in the Co-op as well, although no one could read my signature, and no one there ever asked who the photographer was. The gallery owners had recommended I limit the number of prints to twenty for each print I sold. It allowed them to increase the price since a buyer knew the collection was somewhat limited. For that reason, it didn't make sense to put the limited-edition prints up at a heavy discount in the Co-op, but I sometimes couldn't resist. I liked the idea of my neighbors being able to buy the occasional picture and hang it on their wall. I also didn't mind that they owned something that was about ten times the value they purchased it for in the Co-op.

As I signed photographs and packed them into portfolios to be delivered, I called my dad and put the phone on speaker.

"Critter, what's up?" my dad's voice rang out in the

quiet room.

"Hi, Dad. Is it clear?" It was awful to have to ask that questions but I didn't want to make things worse by letting my mom know I was checking up on her.

"Totally clear. She's taking a nap. She's doing all right today. No need to worry."

"She's really okay? Nothing lingering?"

"She's better." His voice was muffled, and I knew he was moving away from their room in case my mom woke up. "You know how it is. It'll take a while for her to pull out of it all the way. And she's embarrassed that Mark saw some of it this time."

"Dad, I know this is old news, but I really think she needs to see someone." I forced myself to ease up on the special pen I used to sign photos.

"Critter, I wish she would, but you know she's not gonna do that. It's worse again right now because she tried to adjust her medicine."

When I was little, my mom had been prescribed an anti-depressant. Her doctor was content to just keep refilling her prescription without any new real evaluation. My mom tinkered with the dosage far too often and refused to consider maybe she should actually talk to someone or make sure that the medicine was still the right thing.

"Yeah. Okay, Dad." I sighed and attempted to shift the conversation. "How are you?"

"Oh, I'm right as rain, Critter. You know that we're all good here. You take care of yourself. Have a good week and don't work too hard."

"Okay, Daddy. Love you."

∞∞∞

"How about you come over to my place tonight?" Chris asked hopefully.

We'd just finished having another dinner together. It was midweek, and it was all I had been able to squeeze in. He wanted to make plans for the weekend again, and I had to have this talk with him before I was going to agree to an all-day date.

"Chris, I'm sorry. I just don't know if that's a good idea." We were walking along Main Street, and I nudged us in the direction of the park since I knew this might take a while.

"Well, you have to know by now that I'm pretty into you. Crazy about you, really." He squeezed my hand as he affirmed his feelings for me.

"I like you, too. You're sweet and patient." I looked over at him and he looked at me, hungry for more praise. "And funny and good-looking and…"

Chris laughed. "Wow. I'm a catch!"

I laughed as well and said, "Yeah, you really are."

"Well… What's the problem then? Do you just want to go really slow? I mean we are. And we can. But I'd like to move things forward when you're ready."

"See? That's you being sweet again," I said.

We'd reached a tree that was near the lake shoreline. I dropped his hand and put my hand against the trunk to step onto a very low limb. I needed some distance – and something to do to distract myself a little from the intensity of the discussion.

He looked at me with a touch of impatience. I was being confusing. I knew I was.

"Look. Here's the issue. I just think… I think we want two different things." I glanced at his face as he picked at some of the loose bark on the tree.

"Willow, if you're not interested, you could just say –"

"It's not that at all," I assured him. "I like you. I am interested. But you want something I can't give you." I needed to get this out quickly. I knew I was making things worse by making him imagine all the things that could mean. "I don't really do *serious*," I finally said.

"What does that mean?" he asked. "Like you don't do relationships, or you don't want to get married or… Sorry, I don't really understand what you mean."

I leaned back against another branch, trying to read his expression.

"So, yes, I do want a relationship, but I don't want it to be serious. I like going out with you. I'd like to move on to the next step." I spared him a quick glance and saw the hope in his eyes. "But I know that I don't want anything more than that. I really only want *that*. Some dates, some hanging out. Maybe moving on to a… well, a physical relationship."

Chris looked really confused. I knew it was unusual. Didn't my mom tell me that every day? That I was supposed to want love and marriage and a family?

"Look, I just can't do the emotional stuff. I'm happy to be with one person – a relationship, I guess – but I can't do the love stuff. The planning. The future. That's not for me."

"That stuff just takes time, Willow. Maybe you don't want it now, but in time –"

"No, see? That's what I'm worried about. I don't want to lead you on. To make you hope this is going somewhere different than it is. I know myself. This is how I am. I know I'm not going to get where you seem to want to go, and I don't want to lose our friendship."

Chris's expression said everything I needed to know. He was disappointed, hurt, disbelieving. It really didn't matter what he said with words at this point. I had my answer. He was looking for more, and I couldn't give him that.

"You're not going to lose our friendship. Really. I'm okay with this – as long as we're only dating each other. That's what you mean, right? I can be happy with just that. I mean that's enough. I just want to spend time with you."

"Chris," I said, hopping down from the little limb to face him directly. "It's no good. It's just not going to work out. I'm so sorry. I wish it was different." He wasn't looking at me, but I could see his clenched jaw as he looked down at the ground. "I wish I was different."

His expression transitioned from hurt to anger, and when he looked at me, it was with dark eyes, a harsh squint to them. "Our friendship is what you're trying to protect, is that it?"

I tried to reach for his hand, but he jerked it back toward himself.

"I think you have taken care of that, stringing me along for months and then telling me it's not going to work out."

"Look, Chris. I know it's confusing. I'm so sorry. I wasn't trying to string you along. I was enjoying myself, and I thought you were, too. I was trying to see if we wanted the same things, but I was realizing that we really didn't, so I wanted to talk – "

"Enough," he said, looking into the distance over my shoulder. "I think we're actually done here. Your car's just up the road, right? I'm going to take off. See you around, Willow."

With that he set off back toward Main Street.

I stood there, realizing it was the same result no matter what I tried. I was just wired strangely. No one wanted what I did. No one liked to skate by in an emotionless relationship. I definitely lived in "it's not you, it's me" territory, and it looked like I was going to live there by myself.

Chapter 6

I wasn't prone to panic attacks, but I thought there might be a first time for one as I sat in my car, looking at the reception building for Spruce Lake Music Camp. This was so far from my comfort zone. It was like all my deepest shame about my value when viewed through the lens of people who had money, status, education – all of it – was going to break wide open in front of everyone today.

Ruthie came out of the building, waving to me. Indicating they were all waiting for me. I took in a fortifying breath and unfolded myself from my little hatchback. I picked up my bag, which held my computer and documents that I hoped would end my involvement in this weird universe very quickly.

I'd prepared vendor lists with cross-referencing by

location and specialty. I'd also tried to anticipate some of the ideas they were likely to be kicking around. Ruthie had mentioned food ventures. Anthony had asked about wholesale opportunities. This camp had the facilities for events and for a regular restaurant if they wanted to go that direction during the off season.

I knew of a few people in the area who ran food trucks and catering. Some of them also had services available when area farms or organizations would host a harvest dinner – either as a celebration or a fundraiser. I'd created a master spreadsheet that had the vendor list, a resources tab with the caterers and food preparers, as well as an initial shot at projections for revenue if the camp were to open a weekend-only, off-season restaurant and make the venue available for events like weddings. I had two versions of the spreadsheet prepared – one with and one without the projections. I didn't know yet whether offering that information would advance my cause of withdrawing from this endeavor as quickly as possible or make Anthony laugh at my small-town business sense. Or both. I just wanted to have all the preparation I could in my back pocket in case it would move things along so I could get back to my regular life.

"Willow, this is exactly what I was looking for!" Ruthie gushed.

There were four of us sitting around a small conference room table. Ruthie had introduced me to Emerson, the camp Executive Director. And, of course, Anthony sat at the table, looking very authoritative in his expensive business casual attire. This was a glimpse of the real man. The man who had run the multi-million-dollar family business I'd googled after Ruthie had told me about it. This is the man I'd seen society pictures of in eastern seaboard newspaper and magazine sites. There had been an uptick in coverage when he'd sold the business, so there was no shortage of recent pictures. I was curious why he'd sold such a successful company, but I knew it was none of my business so tried to let the curiosity dissipate.

Emerson, who looked like a librarian version of Emma Stone, smiled tentatively.

I had shared the projections in the end. The conversation had quickly become about the ideas they had, which were, indeed, events and a possible eatery of some kind. I saw the opening to getting the heck out of there and had quickly given them printouts and opened my laptop to show how they could use the tool I offered to email them.

Anthony had remained silent. I could feel the judgement rolling off him. Of course, this was small time for him, but I did have a sense of what might work for this area, so if it could help Ruthie and Emerson, I was okay sharing it and extricating myself from the project.

"I really like the idea of the restaurant being a pop-up or occasional thing," Emerson said. "It's a relief that direction might actually be more profitable. That would allow us to keep the few events booked that we already have on the calendar. There are a couple of local chamber music groups that use our venue for concerts in the off season."

"This idea is intriguing, Willow," Ruthie said, pointing to the paper in front of her. "What kind of off-season camps were you thinking about?"

"Oh," I said, not thinking I would be pulled into

this level of planning. "I'm not sure exactly. I haven't seen everything, so I was just imagining some ideas, but since you were asking me from a food perspective, I guess I was thinking maybe the camp could host long weekend camps for would-be farmers or people interested in sustainable agriculture. The local farmers could come in and host some workshops and demonstrations and the producers could supply the food for the weekend. Something along those lines. I know it doesn't seem like there would be much money in it, but we get a lot of tourists who comment about that lifestyle being their dream job. I know it doesn't usually result in anything, but they spend time with Nancy over at Landry Realty, having her show them farmland that's for sale before they go back to the regular lives. Maybe they would see this as a way to keep dabbling in the dream, even if they don't end up ever doing anything more."

"That's not a bad idea," Anthony said, reluctantly. "Capitalize on the hobby farmer idealism that's out there."

"Right," I said. "The hobby farmer idealism." Not

quite how I would have described it, but I guess it was accurate enough.

"Well," Emerson said, standing from the table. "Farming definitely isn't my area, but it sounds like it is something promising to explore. I'd also like to talk about ideas that tie to classical music. I mean, I guess there doesn't have to be crossover, but it would be nice to utilize our music facilities as well. Can I show you all around now, so you'll know what I mean?"

I stood as well and began gathering my things. "I don't think you need me anymore at this point. You all know much more about the rest than I do, but it was very nice to meet you, Emerson. I hope something works out soon."

"Oh, no," Emerson said. "Please don't leave yet. I'd like to show you around and see if that sparks any other thoughts. If you don't mind, that is."

I looked at the petite woman who'd expressed her passion for her cause in a way that I had to admire. When Ruthie had introduced her, Emerson had spoken with quiet enthusiasm about the students and teachers at the camp and the value of spending summers bonding together over classical music while improving their skills. She'd explained that it could be a pretty isolating experience for kids since it was outside the norm.

I hadn't thought of it that way before. I'd really only considered that classical music seemed like something rich people valued. Something that rich people did. But it was true that when I was in school, it wasn't an interest that would have impressed anyone. Football, basketball, baseball... Those were the extracurricular interests that had been valued at my school.

Ruthie looped her arm through mine and began guiding me from the room. "Have a look around, Willow. You're here now. What can it hurt?"

∞∞∞

"So, you never played an instrument, Willow?" Emerson asked as we walked across the expansive lawn to the dining hall.

"No. Well, yes, but like every kid does. I played the

flute for a few years in school band. Through middle school or so." I'd had to stop playing in band like I had stopped taking ballet lessons when I realized my dad could really use my help around the farm. And it seemed like every time I had a dance recital, it was an issue because there was always money needed for costumes. My dad tried to act like it wasn't a big deal, but, even then, I could tell it was stressful.

"And you, Mr. Kaplan?" Emerson asked, shyly looking up at him.

"Anthony, remember?" He gave her the charming smile he'd been flaunting all over town for the last few weeks.

"Right. Anthony," she corrected herself. "Do you play anything?"

"Not anything like this," he said.

"Oh, don't be modest, Anthony. It doesn't become you," Ruthie said as she lightly slapped his arm. "Anthony plays the guitar," she said looking from Emerson to me.

"I noodle around on the guitar," Anthony corrected. "I have a feeling that's not what Emerson is talking about."

"Sure, it is," she said, her eyes brightening as they did every time the conversation shifted to music. "The guitar is a beautiful instrument."

"Yeah, well. I strum. Play some chords. There are a couple of fingerstyle pieces that I keep messing around with, but that's really what it is. Messing around. But it's relaxing – when I can allow myself to not be frustrated by it."

"Yes!" Emerson said. "I know that tension well – relaxing and frustrating."

"Your instrument is the violin, right, Emerson?" Ruthie asked.

"Yes. Yes, the violin."

Emerson pushed the door open to reveal a large dining hall that gave off major lake cabin vibes. The walls were natural wood with vaulted ceilings that had exposed beams with ceiling fans dropping from long downrods. I imagined a hundred or so kids here in the summer and could appreciate the need for the fans. The lake side of the hall had large windows and a deck with tables outside overlooking the lake.

"Isn't it beautiful?" Ruthie asked me.

"Yes, it really is," I said. My appreciation for lovely things was sparked, and I felt pings and zips of excitement dancing through me.

My feelings must have been evident on my face because I could feel Emerson warm to me. I could see Anthony watching me in my peripheral vision, but I'd been doing my best to ignore him. Emerson leaned in and excitedly said, "We have a full commercial kitchen just this way."

The tour continued from there. I saw the beauty, but Anthony saw the problems. Around the cabins, he mumbled about wood rot. When we were looking at the outdoor performance stage, he commented on some weak support posts.

As we walked back toward the reception building, I asked about the small buildings scattered throughout the grounds.

"Oh," Emerson said. "Those are practice huts! Here, I'll show you. We have a teacher who stayed behind for a few weeks after our last camp session ended. I think she usually uses the one closest to the lake."

We walked to the little structure, and I could hear the piano more clearly as we approached. It reminded me of the music that played when we had warmed up at my ballet lessons. I guess ballet and classical music fell into the same upper-class category, but it had never felt that way to me. Where I'd taken lessons was in an older lady's garage that had been converted into a studio. She'd been a dancer in New York years before, but, after a short career, had ended up living in a small house in rural Maine with her husband and had spent the last several decades teaching little kids how to plié and relevé.

Emerson stepped onto the little set of stairs that led into the small building and motioned for us to follow. The room was big enough to hold a piano, a few music stands, and three small chairs. The woman playing had her back to us and continued until she finished the piece. I felt the zips and pings again. Beautiful music in a beautiful setting. It was definitely different than turning on the radio.

"Margaret, hi," Emerson said. "That was beautiful. I love Amy Beach."

"I do, too," the woman replied. "But sometimes my fingers disagree." She smiled at our little group. "Hello."

Emerson made some short introductions, and, after visiting a few more points of interest, we finished our tour. I was more than ready to leave. Music like this in this place was emotional, and I didn't like to do emotional in front of other people.

"Well," Emerson said. "What did you think? Any other ideas?"

"It's a beautiful spot," I said. "I think there are several people on the list I gave you who would love to get some time in that kitchen. And they would be fantastic, but they're all really busy. Maybe they could do some sort of rotating weekend pop-up or something like that? And I'll keep thinking about any other possibilities. I think you are in safe hands with Ruthie, but I'll pass along any ideas to her if I have any."

I started to walk toward my car, and Ruthie and Emerson continued working out some details as I walked away. I was reaching for my door when I heard Anthony's voice behind me.

"Impressive, isn't it?"

"Yes," I said, pulling my door open.

"That's it? Just 'yes'?" His eyes were assessing, calculating. "You had a lot more to say when we were all together."

"I was trying to help. I don't think you're in need of any help from me."

We stood in silence. Anthony didn't seem bothered, but I found it awkward, so I finally said, "I don't really have anything else to say."

"What is it with you not wanting to say what you like? What you think?"

"I'm sorry, what?"

"You heard me."

This smug guy. "What is it with you wanting me to?" I asked.

"Just trying to be friendly," he said.

Friendly! "And I'm not friendly?" I sputtered. "That's what you're saying?" I was frustrated that nothing could be easy with Anthony Kaplan, and I moved away from him to slide my bag in the car and sink into the driver's seat. He grabbed the door before I could close it.

"You're friendly enough. With almost everyone." He

raised his eyebrows significantly. "But I guess I meant something more. We keep running into each other, and now we have this connection through my aunt. I mean – it's just sort of the next step, right? People start saying more than 'hi' or 'hello' at some point. Your friendliness skates on the surface. No one ever called you out on this before? I mean, you're close to my aunt, right? Or you should be. But she said that was the first time you've ever even been to her house. And you've worked with her for how long? I find it hard to believe you don't know what I'm talking about."

Of all the people to push my buttons… My friendliness was always enough for everyone else. No one needed real feelings from me. I gritted my teeth, beyond irritated, and said, "You might want to move your hand before you find it hard to believe I shut the door on your fingers."

He lifted his hands up in surrender as his lips and eyebrows quirked up. I slammed the door and drove away.

Chapter 7

I could tell everyone in the store was walking on eggshells around me. I felt bad; it wasn't like me to show any of my emotions, especially at the store. But Anthony calling me out on... on... basically on my personality. It made me angry. I was refilling some of the bulk containers in our grain aisle and taking out my frustration by slamming the lids as I refilled each one. Customers and co-workers were giving me a wide berth.

Anthony was coming in this afternoon, and, clearly, I wasn't looking forward to it. My week had pretty much been "wash, rinse, repeat." The store was busy. Brendan was not doing any better, and I just didn't have the strength to do anything about it. Working harder myself was an easier solution for the moment. I'd done some more work on replenishing prints for the two galleries and some for the Co-op. There continued to be an uptick in sales for my photos at the store, and I tried to be happy about that. I'd done a few weeknight visits to my parents to try to help reassure my mom that everything was fine… that she was fine. Even though she wasn't. She was on the edge of another meltdown. I was still itching to get some time in the woods. To release some of my anger and get back to my balance.

Who was Anthony Kaplan to judge how I interacted with people anyway? I'd never had any complaints before. So what if I didn't share every feeling or opinion I had? There was something to be said for going with the flow. For letting other people take the lead. For keeping how I felt to myself. I liked my life just fine, and I didn't need to wallow in my feelings or, worse yet, share them with the whole world in order to satisfy him. If other people wanted to do that, good for them.

So, the week was the usual, except for this undercurrent of anger I was feeling – an unusual emotion for me. It was messing with my ability to go with the flow as I usually did. It was making me think about myself and how I was feeling more than I liked to.

And I had to meet with the jerk later in the afternoon. I couldn't wait.

Emerson was considering some of the bigger camp ideas, but, in the meantime, a decision had been made to do a test weekend popup restaurant. Both Emerson and Ruthie had asked if Anthony and I could work together to arrange it while they focused on some grant writing they were in the middle of to try to cover some of the needed facilities improvements Anthony had said were necessary right away.

He'd suggested we meet over dinner. I'd told him I had a half hour in the afternoon if he came to the store. He'd grumbled his consent to the idea, clearly hating that he didn't have the same control over me that he seemingly had over everyone else he interacted with.

When he arrived, I was in the back having another conversation with one of our home bakers who supplied bread for the store. Her bread was popular, but she was unreliable, which made for irritated customers. I got it. This was a home business for her. She obviously had other obligations, like the three small children she was raising. But we needed to find a schedule that worked for her and for the Co-op. We needed a little more of a pattern to her deliveries. Brendan had popped his head in to let me know Anthony had arrived and was waiting for me in the café. I'd nodded and held up a finger, indicating I would be out as quickly as I could. It was hard to even get this baker on the phone, so I wasn't going to blow my one opportunity to finish up a conversation with her.

By the time I made my way out to the café, I was about five minutes late for our arranged time. Anthony looked relaxed, talking to some customers about the weather. *Who's surface-level now, Mr. Perfect?* I thought as I approached.

When he noticed me, I saw a flicker of irritation on his face, and he glanced at his watch.

I rolled my eyes and made a beeline for the coffee thermoses. I sighed as I tried two of the three thermoses to find they were empty. I looked around for Brendan but didn't see him nearby. I rinsed the thermoses and started filling the coffee maker basket with coffee grounds I pulled from the cabinet underneath. The process took another three minutes of Mr. Important's time, which he filled by continuing his conversation while looking at me frequently enough to express his irritation.

Just as I had filled a cup of coffee for myself after getting the first of the two thermoses replenished and had started to walk toward Anthony's table, Brendan approached and informed me the toilet was clogged… again.

Anthony and the two customers he had been talking to looked up when they heard Brendan's notice that he might as well have announced over the PA system. I put my coffee down on the nearest table and went to deal with the problem. I'd called a plumber several times, but I was having a hard time getting anyone scheduled. They were booking out weeks ahead and could only come immediately if there was an emergency.

"Brendan," I complained as he watched me plunging the toilet, "how are you handling this on the days I'm not here?" It was on the tip of my tongue to tell him he needed to take care of it himself, but it was hard for me to delegate crap tasks – pun intended. This was one of those tasks that I felt no one should really have to do, which meant I did it myself.

"Well, you're pretty much always here," he said. "Last weekend, it was a problem, but then you stopped in to check on things and fixed it."

I gagged as a little progress was starting to show.

"You need to call a plumber," Anthony said from behind Brendan.

I froze and felt my face flame. I couldn't remember a time when I had been this embarrassed.

"Yeah, Willow," Brendan chimed in. "When are you gonna get a plumber to come fix this?" I looked up and saw Brendan's carefree grin as the toilet made some humiliating yet promising sounds as it began clearing.

The energy I had left drained away along with the disgusting toilet, and I resolved to ignore my audience. I put away the plunger and started spraying everything down with disinfectant while warming up the water in the sink to burning hot.

"Did you really need to get Willow for this?" I heard Anthony ask Brendan and looked up in time to see the smile slip from Brendan's face. "Is this seriously something you need her to do for you?" Anthony's voice was hard.

"Willow always does it," Brendan defended himself. "Don't you, Willow? You have the magic touch, right?" He pulled his grin back together and tried to make light of the event.

"Would the two of you mind taking this somewhere else?" I asked as I began to close the door, inching them outside the opening. I could hear them murmuring to each other as I scalded my hands and dried them. Anthony's voice low and serious, Brendan's high and defensive.

I waited until they moved away from the door and tried to gather as much composure as I could before returning to the café area, dumping out the lukewarm coffee, and reaching to get a new cup.

"I just got you one," Anthony said from the small table where he sat, two steaming mugs of coffee in front of him.

I moved to take the seat across from him and thanked him without meeting his eyes.

"So, that's the management problem Aunt Ruth was talking about? That kid?"

"It's fine," I said, burning my tongue on the eager sip I took.

"Right," he said. "Well, let's make the most of the few minutes we have before another crisis pops up." He pulled a slim laptop from the messenger bag that was hanging from the back of his chair.

A half hour later, we had an outline of a plan for a weekend pop-up restaurant at the camp in early October. It didn't give us a lot of time, but we needed to get things moving while there were fall tourists in and out of the area.

I'd agreed to work out who would run the kitchen for the weekend, and Anthony was going to work on theme, marketing, and music. He thought Emerson might have some ideas about local musicians who could provide dinner music. The camp didn't have a liquor license which Anthony saw as a big problem, so the marketing for now would have to include a BYOB message. He was working on that type of license, which could be obtained much more quickly than a full liquor license could be.

As we were wrapping up, Brendan approached us, but

Anthony gave him a warning look and Brendan put his hands up and turned on his heel.

"You're going to have to fire that kid," he said to me.

I sighed at how quickly Brendan changed his behavior with just a look from Anthony.

"That *kid* needs the job. I promoted him because he's been struggling since he had to drop out of college. He couldn't afford to keep up his portion of the tuition, and his rent keeps going up. He assured me he'd step up and take on more responsibility if I would promote him. It's just going to take some time."

"This is business. You can't take his personal life into consideration."

"This is *my* business. Or at least my business to run. And I can take anything into consideration that I want to. There aren't a lot of opportunities around here. I want to give him a shot to get better."

I stood up, trying to urge Anthony to do the same and leave. But, instead of standing to leave, he stood to shout out, "Chris!"

I looked to the nearby door where Chris was trying to make a quick escape. We'd been avoiding each other since our last conversation in the park.

"Anthony," Chris said in a low tone as he approached the table. "Willow," he said, catching my eye for a moment.

We stood in awkward silence, Anthony looking between us with a confused expression on his face.

"Well, catch you all later," Chris finally said once it was clear none of us had anything else to say to each other.

"Sure. Later, Chris," Anthony said.

Once Chris made his escape, Anthony looked at me with an eyebrow raised in question. "So, no weekend kayaking plans?' he finally asked.

"Not that it's any of your business," I said, "but no. No plans."

"In that case," Anthony pushed his chair under the table and collected our empty cups. "Why don't we meet up at my place this weekend to see where we are on these restaurant details?"

"Your place?" I asked, horrified. "I think we're good to update each other by email. I don't see any need to meet up."

"I've learned already. If someone doesn't book time with you, you have no time. If we don't set up an appointment, I'll have to pester you for an update, which will annoy you," he said, his eyes gleaming a bit. He looked like a little boy enjoying himself as he pulled my pigtails. "Better to set up a time and place. I'll text you my address."

"Fine," I grumbled, knowing I hadn't given him my number.

"I'll get your number from Aunt Ruth." He winked at me, then placed our cups in the dish bin next to the coffee station. "I do really love those photos," he said, cocking his head to the side and pointing at the latest picture I'd hung in the café area. The one of the beaver dam. I reminded myself he was an ass as I watched him leave the store.

Chapter 8

I was going to cry. It was actually going to happen. It wasn't like I never cried, but when I did, I did it in the comfort of my own home. Not in a waiting room at the hospital.

I was supposed to be at Anthony's in thirty minutes, and I was going to be late. If I made it at all. I didn't know how bad it was yet. I pulled up his contact that I now had in my phone since he'd gotten my number from Ruthie.

Me: I'm not sure if I'll be on time today. I'll update you as soon as I know my ETA.

Anthony: It's the weekend, Willow. You're not supposed to be working, and this is the reason we made a plan.

Me: I'm not at work.

Anthony: … ?

Me: I'm just delayed. I'll let you know.

Anthony: This is what I was talking about. Just tell me. It's the toilet at the store again, isn't it?

Me: Fine. My mom's at the hospital. I'm here waiting to see how she is.

I regretted hitting send as soon as it was done. This was most definitely not his business. Not anyone's business.

The dots appeared and disappeared before Anthony finally replied.

Anthony: Damn. I'm sorry. Sorry I was giving you a hard time. Is there anything I can do? Anything you need?

Me: No. I'm fine. I'm putting away my phone now. I'll let you know if I'm coming later.

I put my phone in my bag and kicked myself for sharing with him. How was I going to explain this one?

"Willow Miller?" A nurse called into the waiting room.

I stood and walked to her, and she gave me a soft, sympathetic smile. "Your mom is fine, honey. She's just this way. Your dad thought it would be good if you came back, too."

She pulled the curtain open, and I saw my mom on the hospital bed sleeping. My dad was in a chair next to the bed, looking exhausted.

"Hey, Dad. How is she?" I approached and was relieved the nurse shut the curtain and left the space.

"She's alright, Critter. The doctor says it looks worse than it is." My mom had scrapes all down her right arm. The right side of her face was swollen and starting to bruise, and she had a busted, fat lip.

"What happened, Dad?"

"She... Well, she fell out of the car."

I gave my dad a doubtful look. "She fell out of the car," I said, letting him know with my tone that I didn't believe him. "And her seat belt didn't keep her in the seat?"

He looked tortured.

"Okay. One step at a time," I said, backing up. "Is she really okay? Did she hurt anything seriously?"

"No, no. Nothing broken. They took some scans and did some tests. We're still waiting for results on some of them, but they don't think there are any internal issues. She's just... just banged up."

I let out a breath. "Okay. Okay, that's good."

My dad lowered his eyes. "Critter, you can't say anything," he said as quietly as he was capable of. She's terrified they're going to make her stay and see new doctors and change her medicine. But she... Well, she didn't fall out. She was upset. Still upset. She said I would be happier without her, and she opened the door and sort of..."

"She jumped out of the car, Dad? Is that what you're saying?" I looked at my mom, bloody and bruised, but sleeping peacefully for a change.

"She didn't really jump. She did fall - kind of. She just made it happen, I guess. It doesn't even make sense. I'd just pulled out from a stop sign, so we were barely moving. But none of it ever makes sense." He looked over at my mom. He was sniffling, trying not to cry. "I just don't understand it."

This wasn't the first time something like this had happened, unfortunately. She threatened often enough. But the few attempts she'd made were always senseless

— like marching deliberately to the hair dryer and threatening to plug it in and put it in water, announcing her intentions every step of the way. The half-hearted attempts were usually easy to stop, and she always ended up in the same tearful place.

"She needs help, Dad. She *needs* to stay here."

"No!" he said, the resolve on his face clear. "That would kill her."

I wasn't sobbing, but I had a few stray tears that had escaped and were running down my cheeks. When my dad and I looked at each other and really took in what he'd just said, we started laughing.

There was nothing else to do, really. It was what it was. And we were used to it.

∞∞∞

An hour later, I made my way out to the parking lot of the hospital. All the tests had come back negative. My mom was still sleeping from the medication they'd given her, and my dad was going to wait until she was awake to get her in the car and take her home. He'd insisted he didn't need my help, and we both knew it would probably be more upsetting to my mom if I was there when she woke up fully and had to face what had happened. What she had done.

I was in a fuzzy place in my head – not really processing thoughts when I heard, "Is she okay?"

I looked up and saw Anthony next to my car. He was leaning against a large black SUV.

"What are you doing – "

"Is she all right?" he asked again.

"She's… she's fine." I began digging in my bag for my keys.

"And you? Are you all right?" He reached out and took my bag from me, pulling the keys fully out that I'd just put my hand on.

"I'm okay. I'm fine. Sorry. Sorry I didn't text back. I just… I just didn't know how long it would be until now."

"Willow, it's okay. You don't need to apologize. I was just worried. I wanted to know if everything was okay. I hadn't heard back and didn't want to blow up your phone, so I thought I'd come check."

"That's… weird. Nice, but weird."

"That's me, I guess. Nice but weird," he smiled his sparkling smile and clicked my key to unlock my car. He opened the door and reached in to place my bag on the passenger seat. He held the door open for me to get in and asked, "Do you need anything? Is there anything I can do?"

"I'm fine. Really. We can do the meeting now. I'm sorry again I didn't let you know. Sorry that you drove here for nothing. Do you still want to meet at your house or maybe somewhere nearby?"

He tilted his head to the side and studied me. "Willow, we don't need to do this today. You need to take care of yourself. Of your mom."

"I'm fine. Really. My dad is here, and he's taking my mom home soon. Everything is fine. I'm good to go."

"You're sure?" he asked, looking doubtful.

"A hundred percent."

"Okay then. I guess… Follow me."

He handed me my keys and shut the door softly after I got into my seat. I had a brief flash of my mom as I put on my seatbelt and quickly put it out of my mind.

After following Anthony's big SUV down back roads and arriving at a little cabin set back in the woods and down a fire lane, I tried to will my mind into work mode. It's not that I was thinking about my mom really. It was just that blank place that my mind sometimes went when it didn't want to think about anything. I realized I didn't have my computer with me and tried to bring up visions of the sheets I had prepared for today's discussion.

"Willow?" Anthony was standing by my car, having already opened my door.

"Yes. Okay."

He led me into the cabin and guided me to a brown leather chair in front of a massive fireplace and hearth. "Have a seat," he said. "I'm going to make us some coffee. Just black, right?"

"Yes," I nodded, sitting in the oversized chair. He started to walk away but then turned toward the matching leather couch and pulled a plaid blanket from the back of it. He put the cover over my lap and said, "Be right back."

I sat, stunned for just a few minutes before I focused

on where I was. I wasn't going to sit here and be treated like I needed special care – like there was really something wrong. I needed to get my mind out of neutral. I could hear Anthony in the kitchen, and I threw back the blanket and stood quickly, making my way toward the sounds.

"Sorry," I said. "Let me help." He was measuring coffee grounds into a large French press and the electric tea kettle was close to boiling.

"Almost finished," he said, looking at me with a soft expression in his eyes. I was used to friendly Anthony and teasing/harassing Anthony. Even impatient, all-business Anthony. But I wasn't used to soft Anthony. I didn't like it.

"Okay," I said. "Why don't we talk here and then I'll head home?" I situated myself at a small breakfast table at the end of the kitchen. The cabin was rustic but expensive. I looked around and took in the modern appliances contrasting with the massive square logs of the structure. It was cozy and elegant at the same time.

Anthony also looked cozy and elegant, and I wanted to slap myself for noticing. He was wearing a light sweater with blue and grey blocks of color, again highlighting his clear, blue eyes. He had on jeans and brown, leather shoes. He looked warm and big. Cozy like his cabin. And he was being so damn nice and soft. And I didn't need any of it.

"That's fine. We can sit here," he said placing two coffee mugs on the table and turning to grab the full French press.

"Are you worried about your mom?" he asked. "Is she sick? Is that okay to ask?"

"No, no. She's not sick. There was just a little accident with the car. She's banged up, but she's fine." I knew this description was misleading, but I didn't care.

"I'm glad then. I mean, it sounds like it could have been worse, but… You seem really stunned. Are you sure she's okay? Sure you're okay?" He poured steaming coffee into the mugs, and I wrapped my hands around the warm cup, seeking comfort.

"It's okay," he continued. "You can tell me."

I looked at his sincere face. The gleam that was usually there when he was intentionally tormenting me wasn't anywhere to be found. Instead, he was looking at me like he really cared how I was feeling. He had some tension around his eyes, showing his concern. "It's what friends do," he said.

"Friends?" I asked. "You think we're friends?" Maybe I'd been wrong about the tormenting part. Maybe this was another way for him to make fun of my reserve again.

"I think we're going to be. We can start now." He clinked his mug softly against mine in a little toast. "What's going on?" he prodded.

For some inexplicable reason, I suddenly wanted to tell him. Wanted to be at least a little honest about what was going on with my mom.

"My mom… She isn't… she isn't well," I finally said.

Anthony didn't say anything. He just waited patiently for me to continue.

"She suffers from depression. She takes an anti-depressant, but she messes around with the dosage frequently, and she refuses to see anyone. It's not a big deal, but every once in a while, something like this happens."

"Something like… ?" A look of horror slowly took

over Antony's features. "It wasn't an accident? Is that what you mean?"

"She sort of let herself out of the car while it was still moving." Anthony's look of horror morphed into a blank slate of an expression. His poker face, I guessed.

"The car was barely moving, so it's not as bad as it sounds," I continued.

"It doesn't sound great," Anthony mumbled. "Look, this camp stuff can wait. We still have some time, and today is getting on. Why don't I put one of those casseroles in the oven that I bought at the Co-op? And we can watch something distracting on TV. Do you like sports? Cheesy Hallmark movies? Reality TV? I'm good with anything."

And that's how we ended up sitting on Anthony's big leather couch for the next few hours. We didn't need it, but he lit a small fire, and my eyes were on that more than the TV. There was a big screen above the hearth, and we watched a football game. I didn't really follow football, but I watched some with my dad. Honestly, the announcers put me to sleep most of the time, but it was relaxing.

We didn't talk much more. Anthony heated a premade Mexican lasagna and loaded up the coffee table with the casserole, plates, chips, and salsa. He also brought out some wine that I sipped on. I wasn't much of a drinker, but I welcomed the tiny buzz I allowed myself as we sat there. I kept noticing Anthony glancing at me every so often, but I didn't let it bother me. I had done what he wanted. I shared something about myself, and now he was letting me be. He didn't need to sit with my "sorta" secret, but he seemed okay doing it. I had burrowed myself into the arm of the couch and felt snug under the plaid blanket Anthony had given me again.

As I tilted more toward the wall, I noticed one of my photos hanging there. It was a shot I had taken last year at low tide. There was a spot where the rocks were formed into lines – like giant ski tracks – and there were little tidal pools scattered between them. I had taken a close-up shot and washed it in sepia tones. It was on the abstract side for me, but the lines were pleasing, and sepia softened it enough to have the photo make sense in my portfolio.

Anthony caught me looking at the picture. "You like

that one? I have a few more – just waiting to get them back from the framers."

"You're the one buying them up lately?"

"Guilty. There's something special about them. I've been wanting to ask you about the artist –"

I sat up, suddenly feeling uncomfortably exposed.

"But another time," he finished. "Not today."

Once the game ended, I stood to go. Anthony also stood and walked toward me.

"What are you doing?" I asked, confused that his big frame just kept getting closer and closer.

"I'm hugging you, Willow." He reached out and brought me into his hard, comforting chest. His arms engulfed my smaller frame, and he just held me. I breathed in his clean scent. He was a perfect mix of this rustic cabin guy with worldly, put-together businessman. In control. In charge. And he smelled amazing. He squeezed me a bit tighter, and I felt the tears leaking again. I could control myself enough to avoid full-on crying, but I couldn't stop the leaking. "You're okay," he said as he rubbed my back.

I broke the hug and swiped the tears from my cheeks

quickly. "Please don't tell Ruthie," I said, looking up, up, up into his face.

"No chance," he said. "Friends don't share what's no one else's business."

"Thanks. And thanks for dinner. I'm sorry we didn't get things settled for the event."

"Stop worrying, Willow. We have time."

I picked up my keys from the coffee table and headed for the door where my shoes were. I quickly put them on and thanked Anthony again.

"Anytime," he said as I slipped out the door.

Chapter 9

Brendan was doing better, which was actually infuriating. I could not believe that a few words and some stern looks from Anthony had improved Brendan's performance. Nothing else had changed though, so I couldn't think of anything else it could be attributed to. He wasn't going to win employee of the month anytime soon, but he was a little more focused. Taking on a little more responsibility. And, seeing how easily he'd changed made me upset with myself for giving him such a long leash before. For believing that I needed to give him lots of time to ease himself into the new role. I had downloaded some performance review materials and resolved to start holding him (and others in the shop) more accountable.

I'd also re-committed myself to leaving the shop at

more normal times and not checking in – at least not as frequently – on the weekends.

I was enjoying the result of those decisions by feeling caught up with the gallery requests I'd been so behind on and by being able to look forward to a hike in a few days when the weekend arrived. I was planning out my hike as I pulled into the driveway at my parents' house. I had stopped by to see my mom a few times since the "accident" as we were calling it. They were short visits. She was as down as she ever got. There was nothing left of the venom she had during her episodes. She was just weepy. Slow and sad. She was indifferent about my visits. I was glad she wasn't opposed to them, but the indifference brought the usual sting of hurt.

"Mom, are you sure you shouldn't just do one appointment with someone? It might be a tweak to some medication or something that could help."

The three of us sat at their kitchen table, drinking coffee and some pastries I'd brought from the store. My dad was silent.

"No, honey," my mom answered. "It was my fault. I was trying to cut back on the dosage. The medicine is fine. I just have to take it, even it if makes me feel loopy." This was the reason Mom was always trying to adjust her medicine. The tradeoff for not hurling herself from a car was an especially fuzzy head that made her feel stupid and have a hard time keeping up with conversations. It's why she often complained when my dad and I were enjoying each other's company. She felt on the outside of it and believed it was because of her medicine. It likely was.

"Mom, it's been so long. There are all kinds of treatments now. Maybe there's something better. Or maybe if you just talked to someone. You know, that could help, too." I braced for her response. This suggestion usually elicited a strong reaction.

This time though, she just didn't have the energy. "I'm fine, honey. Really. I'm sorry for... everything. I think I'm going to go try to take a nap." She stood and patted my hand. I looked up into her bruised face and felt the thickness in my throat and the water in my eyes.

I turned my hand over to hold hers. "Get some rest, Mom."

She left the kitchen, and I looked at my dad. He

lowered his eyes and fidgeted with his coffee cup. "She won't do it, Critter," he finally said. "I promise I've talked to her about it again. She just won't talk to anyone about it."

"Except you. She talks to you."

"Not enough. And I don't know what to do about it. How to make it better." His voice broke on the last sentence.

"Dad, you do make it better. She adores you, and you are so good with her. Except it also encourages her to stay the same, and that's not fair to either of you. The stuff from when she was little... That's stuff she should be talking to a professional about."

I took in his defeated posture and felt sorry for him. It hurt to feel sorry for him all the time. In some ways, he was the hero lots of dads are to their daughters. He was kind and good. Caring and strong, and I loved him for that. But the role reversal that we had in some instances – the foreclosure, the ongoing finances, my mom – those put me in the parent role, and it felt awful for both of us.

"Okay, Dad," I said. I stood to leave, giving him a side

hug as he sat hunched over the table. "It'll be okay."

∞∞∞

"Why not?" Anthony asked me. I was in the café area of the Co-op, again dreaming about my planned hike the following day.

"Because I'm busy," I said, picking up the bin of dirty coffee cups and carrying it to the kitchen area. Anthony grabbed a second bin and followed me.

"Busy here?" he asked.

"No," I said, starting to put the coffee cups in the dishwasher. Anthony put his bin on the counter and began to do the same from the other side.

"Willow," he said, "we've talked about this. Friends share things. What are you so afraid of?"

"Nothing," I protested. "I'm not afraid of anything. I just don't go around talking about myself all the time."

"Well, you should. At least a little more. So what is it? Hot date?" he asked. I startled a little as the cup he dropped in the dishwasher rattled loudly. "Going to visit your mom?" he asked more gently.

"No and no," I said, softening at how kind he continued to be about my mom. "I'm going on a hike. I've been looking forward to it all week. I can meet with you about the Spruce Lake event on Sunday maybe. Or early next week."

"Or… " Anthony stopped loading the cups until I looked up at him and gave him my attention. "We could go together on the hike and talk about the event while we're at it. Two birds, one stone."

It should have been the last thing I would have wanted. I'd been planning a working hike – I wanted to get some pictures taken. Wanted some time with my own thoughts. But it increasingly felt good to be around this man. The only thing he ever pushed me about now was to ask me to share more about myself. But, once I did share something, he wasn't demanding. He didn't criticize or tell me to be different. He just listened and took it in. It felt pretty good to have someone who gave a damn but didn't actually want anything from me. I thought again that those were the traits he had that would have made him the perfect casual relationship partner. If only he weren't so far out of my league. It would be nice to be with someone like him. Casually. But the friend thing was good, too. I had plenty of friends. Or people who I thought of as friends – and they thought of me as a friend. But really, we were just friendly, I guess. I didn't share much about myself – my real self – with them, and I certainly didn't ask probing questions about them. I was starting to be happy that he had pushed past a little of my reserve. The friend thing was nice.

"It's a good idea," he said, sensing I was persuadable.

"Okay. Fine," I said, "but Sunshine is coming."

"I wouldn't have it any other way."

∞ ∞ ∞

I tried to stop laughing, but I just couldn't. Rich, successful, beautiful Anthony was ridiculously impersonating his aunt.

"Loren, we need to fit in a trip to the food bank and the battered women's shelter before the hospital charity ball. The coordinator at the food bank set aside a donation for the shelter, but the regular volunteer driver is sick

today and they don't have anyone to transport it. The coordinator is only available from 3:45 until 4:00 and the person at the shelter who knows what to do with the delivery will be leaving at 4:00, so we have to make the timing work. Oh, and your tux is still at the dry cleaners, so we have to pick it up ahead of time. I just need to finish this speech for the ball and then we can get going. They asked me to stand in for the keynote speaker at the last minute."

Anthony's hands gestured wildly as he exaggerated all the vowels in his speech as Ruthie had a tendency to do.

"Stop. Please stop," I squealed from my place next to him. We were sitting on a small wooden public dock. Sunshine was looking over the edge at fish near the surface of the water. "It's too much."

"Aunt Ruth is too much, you mean," he said, chuckling. "She's great though. Really the best."

"Yes, she really is," I readily agreed. "And the fact that she thinks all of those things are so normal – it's always surprising to me."

"How long have you worked with her?" Anthony asked as Sunshine approached his outstretched hand.

"She won't jump in, will she?" he asked worriedly, rubbing my cat from her head to her tail.

"No," I said, "She just watches. And as for Ruthie? Years - a decade or so. More, I guess. I started at the Co-op when I was finishing high school." I stretched out flat on my back and looked at the sky above. "She took an interest in me after a year or two of working there, and she encouraged me to look at it as a career when she knew I wouldn't be going to college. She was amazing. Is amazing."

"She is," Anthony said, shifting in preparation to also lean back on the dock. "You're sure the cat's okay?"

"I'm sure," I patted my chest and Sunshine came to me and settled.

Anthony gave a small laugh and eased his big body flat on the dock as well. "I spent a good part of almost every summer here with her and Uncle Loren while I was growing up." He let out a contented sigh. "It was the best part of the year."

"Where did you grow up?" I asked. This was so much easier, talking to the blue sky instead of his blue eyes.

"New York – sort of. My parents lived in New York. I

spent a lot of time at various boarding schools. Some in upstate New York. One in Boston. A year in England on exchange. I came back to Boston though for undergrad. I still consider that to be the place I live for the most part."

"You live there now? I mean, have a house or apartment or something there?"

"Yeah. It's home base for me, I guess."

"What about the business thing?" I asked, feeling free in this friend zone Anthony had created. "Why did you sell? Are you doing something new?"

"I don't know exactly." Anthony reached out to Sunshine who was now tracking back and forth between us. "I was just over it, I think. Since I was young, I've been pushed to succeed – by my parents, then teachers, headmasters, the system really. So, I did. I worked hard, grew the business. Enjoyed parts of it."

"Construction company?"

I could sense him nodding next to me. "We developed commercial properties. Eventually we specialized in hotels, which had an interesting irony for me since I never felt grounded in a physical place. Hotels are for people when they aren't home, and I didn't really have a home in the usual way. So hotels kind of felt friendly to me – like they were a place for me. It was nice to work with the architects and planners on making the spaces feel warm and inviting. It was part of what gave us an edge. When a company was looking for something a little different, they came to us. We worked with a few chains, but most often, we worked with boutique hotels. We were the builders, but I got to be involved in all the planning and development and found myself increasingly interested in the restaurants, cafés, and lobby coffee bars. It was a lot of fun working through those themes and, while I didn't have an active hand in the menu development or chef selection or any of that, I became friendly with all those people and got to informally collaborate. And I guess eventually I realized some of those friends were having more fun than I was. They were living a passion more than I was. I did my job well enough to keep the business growing, but a lot of the people around me were doing things they were passionate about and doing things that I was really more interested in. So I finally asked myself, 'Why am I doing this?'"

Before I could think better of it, I said, "Must be nice to be able to afford to just quit because you weren't having as much fun as you should be."

Anthony didn't say anything, which made me hear my unkind words on repeat in my mind. He'd been sharing how he felt because I'd asked, and I had responded by mocking him.

"Sorry," I said.

"No, I guess that's one way to look at it. I'm spoiled enough to be unemployed and lazy," he said with a defeated huff. "It's nice to finally be clear on what it is you have against me."

"I don't have anything against you," I protested. I watched a cloud slowly creep by and wanted to rewind time.

Anthony scoffed and sat up. I refused to look at him, although I could feel him looking down at me. "Right," he said. "From the first time I saw you in the store, you had it in for me. I couldn't figure it out. You were friendly enough with everyone else, but every time I saw you, it was like you couldn't get away from me fast enough."

"Fine, okay?" My cheeks burned, and I felt like a terrible person. "I did – I *do* have a problem with people who have money." It was childish, but I rolled to my side away from him to look out at the water so he couldn't see my face anymore.

"How can you just have a *problem* with people who have money? What does that even mean? How do you even know?"

"Oh, I know," I said petulantly. "It's obvious with your clothes and your 'everything and everyone caters to me' attitude. It's just an expectation you all have. That the world and everything in it is there for you to take."

"I don't think everything is there for me to take. Dammit, Willow, I've worked hard for what I have."

"So have I," I said. "But we don't have the same things, do we? Even though we both worked for them."

"Right," he said, standing up. "We should probably get going."

Chapter 10

"So October 15th is the day?" Ruthie asked, looking between Anthony and me. We'd been summoned to have coffee with her at High Rise Coffee on an afternoon the following week.

Anthony and I had exchanged some emails about the details we had never gotten around to discussing on our hike or on the silent ride back home. If this was what came from being candid and sharing my feelings, I wanted no further part of that.

I nodded to Ruthie, affirming we'd agreed through email that October 15th would be the date of the first popup restaurant weekend. Then I snuck a glance at Anthony. He didn't look great. I mean, he looked great in the usual way, but he didn't have his usual positive energy. I figured I had done that, and I felt pretty terrible about it.

Honestly, I had no idea I even had the ability to hurt him like that. Why would he care that I thought people with money... that people with money... I stopped and considered as I had done many times since that day. What was I really saying? That people with money didn't deserve it? That people with money were lazy? That they couldn't be nice or hard-working people because of it?

What I really felt was that it was just unfair. Why did some people get all the money, all the luck, all the breaks? And some people didn't get very many of those things? I knew there were other ways life could be unfair, but this one. This bias – I just couldn't make it go away. I still felt strongly that it was unfair, but I felt bad I'd shared that feeling with him.

In answer to more of Ruthie's questions, he was now explaining to her that I'd gotten Luisa Smith to act as chef for that weekend. Luisa was one of Adam Smith's daughters. Adam ran Smith's Dairy, and Luisa had gone out on her own recently to run a lobster roll food truck in the summer. I knew she had solid baking skills as well, so I hoped this would be a good chance for her to expand her experience.

"Time is ticking," I heard Ruthie say. "Are we going to be able to pull it together? I think Emerson could use help this weekend getting things ready. Are you both able to do that?"

I looked at Anthony who was avoiding looking at me. "I'm planning on it," he said.

This was the man who thought I had called him lazy.

"Me, too," I said quietly, ashamed of myself.

Whatever I thought about people with money, I believed Anthony was a kind man who gave far more than he got. He had no reason to care about me (not that he did anymore), support me through that night with my mom's accident, or help his aunt with this project. He could be living it up anywhere he wanted. Instead, he was sitting here, drinking coffee with his elderly aunt and pitching in where he was needed. Ruthie had told me he was even helping Emerson find some corporate sponsorship and grant funding for the facilities improvements he'd recommended, which included support from some foundation he chaired. I was beginning to suspect it was his own foundation and his own money.

Once we worked out a few more details, Ruthie surprised us both by making a quick departure. "I have another meeting, so I have to rush, but you two stay and enjoy the rest of your coffee." She gave me a shoulder squeeze and hugged Anthony who had stood to help her to her feet.

Once she walked away, Anthony began to collect napkins and Ruthie's cup and spoon. "I should get back, too," he said.

"Anthony, please wait," I said before he could make his escape. "Please, just a few minutes."

"What is it, Willow?" he sighed. "I think we have the details under control."

"No, not Spruce Lake. This – you and me. Our *friendship*." My voice faltered on that word – the one he had pushed our relationship into. I couldn't make myself meet his eyes, but I forced myself to continue talking. "I... I'm really sorry I said those things to you. I –"

"Our friendship?" he asked in a contemptuously

hushed voice. "You make a habit of being friends with people you have a *problem* with. A problem based on –"

"No," I said, interrupting him. "No, please sit down. Please? Just a few minutes."

Anthony lowered himself back into his chair, but his face remained wary.

Before he could change his mind, I began speaking quickly. "I don't make a habit of making friends – the kind of friends we were becoming - at all. You've been pushing me to tell you how I feel. I'm not used to doing that, and I did. And it was awful. I'm sorry to say that *is* how I feel. But not about you. And I'm sorry I said it. I can see how hard you work. How much you give. And how kind and generous you are. You're like Ruthie." I finished, searching his face for any understanding. "You're an exception to the rule."

"And the rule is?" His jaw tensed as he awaited my response.

"No rule," I lied. "I shouldn't have said it, and I'm really sorry." I looked at him, pleading with my eyes. "Can you please forgive me? I'm not good at sharing what I think. It's like I am apparently all filter or no filter. I have to learn something in the middle to not just be a jerk like I was."

Anthony settled into his seat a bit more. "I have been pushing you about sharing your thoughts with me. Maybe I shouldn't have done it so much." He lowered his voice to a quiet hush "And what you said about… Well, I'm sorry that it's unfair." He gifted me with his clear blue eyes. "You're right, Willow. You do work hard. I do get what you were saying about that part. And I'm sorry it's like that having different things when we both work hard."

I looked down at the table, embarrassed. "Can we please just forget this whole thing? I don't want to talk about it anymore, except to say I'm sorry again. Is that okay?"

"Okay," Anthony said. He leaned back and crossed his legs at his ankles. His eyes twinkled as he said, "I hear a certain plumber finally showed up at the Co-op."

∞∞∞

"But there's no reason for me to come." I stared at

my phone waiting for Anthony's reply to my text. We were talking about the night before the restaurant opening. Luisa Smith was going to do a test run of her menu for Emerson and a few other Spruce Lake staff and board members. Some of them were going to work as waitstaff, and Anthony had thought this would be a great way for Luisa to get comfortable with the kitchen and the menu and for the people who would be servicing tables (who normally did things like office work or playing music) a chance to do a little preparation as well.

"We need you there," he texted back. "*I'm sure Luisa would like your support, and I know things are going to come up. I'd like your opinion as they do.*"

And that's how I found myself pulling into Spruce Lake again. Things with Anthony had been great since our last meeting. We'd been texting regularly and had spent some time together at the camp with Emerson making sure the space was equipped and ready to go. It had been nice. He wasn't a grudge-holder. Once I'd gotten past my discomfort over the situation, I'd relaxed into Anthony's ease. With my guard down, I was better able to take his teasing as affectionate. I was better able to see that while he was, in fact, a skilled schmoozer, he also genuinely *enjoyed* being friendly with everyone.

"You're such a golden retriever," I said as I made my way out of my car. He was standing next to it waiting for me, smiling.

"And you're a bit of a grumpy cat."

"Me?" I asked in mock indignation. "First, cats are the best and not at all grumpy. They're just reacting to what the world gives them. Second, no one has ever called me grumpy in my life. You do know what it means to be a pleaser, don't you? It's making sure no one ever calls you grumpy!"

"But you're not a pleaser with me." His eyes were shining, and he started to direct me toward the dining hall.

"Well, no. Because I'm reacting to what the world is giving me."

"Right. You're a grumpy cat with me. A cute grumpy kitten."

I looked at the ground and tamped down my grin.

I loved this feeling. I loved that I gave a little more of myself with Anthony than I usually did with anyone else. It felt good to tease and show parts of myself I normally kept hidden.

"I have someone for you to meet," Anthony said as we took the few steps up onto the wraparound porch surrounding the dining hall. There were beautifully set tables on the porch as well as the ones clearly showing through the large windows in the dining hall. I knew Anthony had taken an active role in making sure the hall had a rustic chic look for the opening. We'd been throwing around ideas for more specific themes, but, in the end, the setting, the resources, the people – it all just suited a simple farm-to-table theme, and that's where we had landed.

There were no tablecloths, but the tabletops were thick slabs cut from massive logs, showing all their natural beauty. There were vases of wildflowers and floral cloth napkins. I knew Anthony had selected some simple white dishes to allow the food and atmosphere to be the stars.

"Someone for me to meet?" I asked. I didn't really

like the idea of sharing my friend with anyone. We had Ruthie in common, which was a lovely connection, but I didn't like the idea of sharing him with *his* people. The shiny people in the magazine pictures I'd seen online. The people I absolutely couldn't be any part of myself around.

"Yes," he said simply.

We walked in the door and were immediately accosted. Emerson ran up to Anthony, concerned about an oven hood in the kitchen that wasn't venting properly. Luisa came up to me asking if I could give her a hand in the kitchen. She said she was far behind where she should be and wondered how I'd ever thought she could do this.

Anthony and I parted ways and found ourselves tied up, helping out in different ways for the hours before service was supposed to start.

"Luisa, stop panicking," I said. "Just take a deep breath." We were in the kitchen at the prep station. Her menu consisted of a roasted vegetable salad, an apple walnut stuffed pork roast with a garlicky white bean mash, and individual salted caramel pear trifles for dessert. She had some substitutions she could make to accommodate other food preferences and restrictions, which was the source of her current anxiety.

"I wasn't thinking, and I poured all the vegan caramel in dessert dishes that had regular cake pieces instead of the vegan cake pieces I had made." She miserably gestured to a hotel pan filled with perfectly cut squares of vegan white cake. "There's no way I can re-do this. I have to finish working on the roasted beets for the salads and about a million other things."

"Do you have a recipe for the caramel?" I asked. "You can serve this one as the regular option, and I can do a new caramel for the vegan cake. I'm no great chef, but I can follow a recipe."

"I'm no great chef, Willow! How did you talk me into this? It will just be another fail in a long line of fails."

I didn't know Luisa well, but I guessed she was thinking about a recent divorce she'd gone through. When she had married, her husband was already someone who worked with her dad on her family's farm. I was guessing that had made the breakup particularly hard since the split affected where they all worked. All I really knew was that it hadn't worked out, and Luisa had started her summer food truck shortly after.

"Luisa," I forced her to turn toward me and stop her nervous and useless shifting of various items on the prep bar. "Take a deep breath."

She looked at me with an anxious expression, and I tried to calmly look back at her. "Deep breath," I reminded. She finally took in a shallow inhale, followed by a few more as I modeled the breathing, a little deeper and more relaxed each time.

"Good," I reassured her. "Now jot down your vegan caramel recipe. I can do that and assemble the trifles while you work on the salad and check on your roasts."

As I was opening the can of coconut milk a short while later and watching the vegan butter and maple syrup mixture closely to make sure it was just the right temperature, Anthony came up behind me and said, "You're good at that."

"This?" I asked, indicating my little work area. "I'm just following Luisa's recipe."

"No, not this. Well, yes. It looks like you know what

you're doing on this too, but I meant you're good at calming people down. She was losing her mind."

Anthony and I both looked over at Luisa who was standing at the main stove and workstation. She looked much more confident now – in her element as she prepped a line of plates and her bins with the prepared salad ingredients.

I shrugged. "She just needed a little perspective."

"Which you were good at giving her," he said. "You're kind of always taking care of people from what I can tell."

I thought about my mom and all the times in my life when I'd needed to calm her down and shrugged again. It wasn't something I had considered before.

"This looks delicious," he said as he dragged a piece of the cake through the gently simmering liquid that was progressing into caramel after I had stirred the coconut milk in.

"It will be better if you give it a minute," I laughed, slapping his arm as he blew on the piece of cake he now held near his mouth. "And that caramel is going to burn you!"

He blew on it harder, exaggerating his action by widening his icy blue eyes at me. Then he quickly popped it in his mouth and gave an exaggerated moan.

I laughed and shoved him on his shoulder before returning to my stirring. "That will be the best thing I eat tonight," he said before squeezing my elbow and heading toward the dining room.

I knew he was just joking around, and I had to keep reminding myself of that each time I replayed his reaction as he had closed his eyes for a second.

∞∞∞

"Willow, this is my mother, Sylvia Kaplan. Mom, this is my friend, Willow."

"Nice to meet you," Anthony's mom said, dismissively turning her attention straight back to the people at her table. She was sitting with Ruthie, Dr. Marsh, Anthony, and what I assumed were some Spruce Lake board members.

I hadn't done much sitting at all. Although my official seat was at Emerson's table, that table had been mostly empty all night since Emerson had been busy in the front of the house, and I'd been running back and forth between the front and the back, trying to pitch in where I could.

We'd arrived at the dessert portion of the evening. I hadn't forgotten that Anthony had mentioned he had someone for me to meet. I also hadn't failed to notice the glamorous woman seated at his table, but I hadn't known who she was until now. There wasn't a strong resemblance, but, looking at her closely, I could see that the bleached hair, botoxed face, impeccable but heavy makeup – all of the artificial bits that made up this woman - would hide any natural resemblance anyway.

"Nice to meet you, too," I said to the back of her head. Anthony was standing just behind me, and I was standing to the side of his mother's seat.

"Mother, Willow is the one I was telling you about. She helped get this whole event together and has some good ideas about helping with Aunt Ruth's fundraising goals for this place."

Mrs. Kaplan spared me another glance, looked up at Anthony, and then turned in her chair more fully toward us. Instead of feeling like this was her attempt at being more polite and engaging with me, it quickly became evident that she was turning to assess me. She wasn't discreet in looking me up and down. I had on an oversized baby pink sweater with dark brown pants tucked into my tall boots. I didn't think to dress up more than that. I had to come right after work and knew I would be up and down. I also knew that the vibe we were going for wasn't overly formal. It was evident Mrs. Kaplan, with her impeccable grooming, sparkly jewelry, and form-fitting square neck black dress didn't agree and didn't approve of my appearance.

"That's nice," she said, giving me what bordered on a sneer before looking at Anthony. "Darling, Candice will be here tomorrow. She's so looking forward to seeing how you are coping, roughing it up here with the locals." Mrs. Kaplan's disdain was evident in both her words and her tone.

"It's hardly rough living, Mom. And she'll see – as you can – that I'm coping just fine."

"Anthony, darling, really… It's been long enough. Your little project with Ruth is up and running. Time for you to come back to the city. Candice and I were just talking –"

"Right, Mom. I think they need us in the kitchen." Anthony gripped my elbow and guided me away from the table.

"Sorry about that," he said as we walked into the back. "She can be a lot."

"That's okay," I said, looking around to see if there was something I could do to help in the kitchen. Luisa was slurping down a large glass of water. The desserts were out, and she was taking a well-deserved moment for herself.

"No, it's not okay. She was being rude. And I'm sorry to say it's not entirely out of character for her. I've been able to avoid it most of my life, but since my dad died, she's focused her energy on trying to organize me and my life more. I didn't even know she was coming until yesterday."

"It's totally fine," I said again, wondering about the information he'd just shared about his dad. "How long ago did that happen? With your dad?"

"A few years. Lung cancer. It all happened pretty

quickly."

"I'm sorry." I felt like I should say more, but I didn't know what to say.

Ruthie walked into the kitchen then, clearly looking for Anthony. "Your mother would like to leave, Anthony," she said, irritation clear in her voice. "Do you think you could get her home? It might be better for the board members to not hear more of her opinions about the rustic nature of our 'little corner of the world.'"

"Right," Anthony said, his jaw clenching. "Sorry, Aunt Ruth. I'll get her out of the way."

"Thank you. Willow, will you be able to stay a while? Things went well, but Luisa is a little in over her head considering we will have four times more people at tomorrow's dinner."

"Sure," I said. "Of course."

Anthony gave me an assessing look. "Not too long though. You look a little tired. Let Luisa do the heavy lifting. You have to work tomorrow, too?"

"Of course," I said. "Friday is usually a busy day, but I'm fine. Go on and take care of your mother."

Chapter 11

Anthony was right. I was tired. And the last twenty or so hours hadn't helped matters. I'd stayed late at Spruce Lake the night before helping Luisa get everything cleaned up, and while Brendan was doing better, work was still overwhelming. Even when things in the store ran more smoothly, there were always different vendors to work with, various administrative tasks to catch up on, and a board to keep happy.

Additionally, Ruthie had forced me to issue an invitation to my parents for the Spruce Lake Farm Supper opening. I'd hoped beyond hope that my mom would refuse. The odds on her reaction to things like this were fifty-fifty. She didn't really like people and could be volatile around them, but, on the other hand, she liked attention. She liked for people to notice her.

My mom hadn't made up her mind until close to the last minute, and I started getting phone calls from her late in the afternoon at work. She wanted to know what other people would be wearing, what time they should show up, if there was a place to park where they wouldn't attract any negative attention arriving in their older truck. While she loved my dad and genuinely thought he was the best – with all his back woods ways included – she often forgot how much none of that bothered her personally when she felt others looked down on it.

I was trying to finish my work while taking calls from her every fifteen minutes. I hadn't had time for anything to eat and was running on coffee as I had been mostly for days. I was hoping I would get a chance to actually eat the lovely meal tonight. I hadn't gotten much opportunity at the test run the night before.

Not wanting to invite the same disdain for my appearance from Anthony's mom – or my own, for that matter – I'd brought one of my nicer dresses to work with me and I spent a few minutes in the tiny office trying to get ready for the event before leaving work. I cared about the project now – was truly invested - but I was finding it difficult to muster the energy I really needed to get ready and feel excitement for Emerson, Ruthie, and Luisa. This was a hopeful, and possibly pivotal, event for all of them. I continued to remind myself of that as I pulled a dark green sweater dress over my head.

The dress had a v-neck and was belted with a soft flair that ended a few inches above my knees. I wore black tights and low-heeled buckled Mary Jane pumps. Not half as elegant as Anthony's mother had been dressed the night before. Or Emerson and her colleagues for that matter. But it was dressy for me. I ran a brush through my hair and decided to make my mother happy by applying some mascara and lipstick.

Rushing from the store to my car, I ran into Chris. I tried to greet him, but he completely ignored me. Sighing at yet another loss of a sort-of friendship, I gathered any energy reserves I had left and made my way toward Spruce Lake.

∞∞∞

Upon arrival, I quickly realized I'd been ridiculously naïve to think I might get to sit and enjoy the meal for any length of time. There were twelve different crises happening in the kitchen. In the dining room, too, for that matter, but Anthony, Emerson, and Ruthie were all there to smooth those over.

Luisa had a couple of helpers, but she wasn't used to running a kitchen and delegating. Her helpers were trying to be busy but were mostly at a loss as to how to best help her. The prep in the kitchen was not as organized as it should have been for the eighty or so diners that would be served that evening. The components were ready, but they were scattered at different ends of the kitchen, and she didn't have a workable plan for heating and assembly. After helping her sort through the steps that were going to be needed, we crafted a plan, gave some instructions to the two helpers, and got the kitchen in order. I took on the role of expediting orders because I didn't see how things would actually leave the kitchen otherwise.

I was standing at the warming table, wiping dinner plates when Anthony swept into the kitchen looking more appealing than the beautiful plates of food we were (despite all the obstacles) sending out. He was in a dark brown suit that fit him like a glove. Emerson was just behind him looking beautiful in a camel colored, safari style dress. Her strawberry blonde hair was perfectly skimming her shoulders, her face was energetically flushed, and her eyes were bright.

I, on the other hand, had a dirty apron covering my dress, my hair up in a messy bun held together with a literal rubber band that I'd found discarded in a vegetable box, and I was sweaty. All over.

"Are you doing okay, Willow?" Anthony asked.

"Everything is going so well!" Emerson exclaimed. "The food is incredible!" she called to Luisa who was working away behind me. "Everyone is raving. And thank you so much, Willow! I can't believe how this has come together."

"Willow," Anthony addressed me again, "maybe I could take a turn doing this so you could take a break?"

"No, I'm fine," I said, glancing at his perfect suit. "You would get all dirty, and they need you out there." I pushed the three finished plates forward toward one of the helpers who was running plates out to the diners. She took the food, and Emerson followed her out to the dining room again.

"Willow, really. Are you okay? I'm happy to take a turn. You should get something to eat and sit for a few minutes." He started to take off his suit jacket when Ruthie came through the doors.

"Anthony, we need you out here. The CEO of that lumber company has arrived. Time to peddle those important connections of yours. We need a discount on materials for the repairs to the outdoor stage."

"Give me a few minutes. Willow could use a break."

"No, Anthony. I'm fine. Go. It's important."

He looked at me again, clearly torn. I soaked in the sweet concern he was showing for me and determined to help finish this night on a high note.

"Really, go," I said, shooing him toward the door. "It'll be easier for me just to finish this off myself. I can take a break in a bit when we get to dessert. Those are already made and ready to go out."

Anthony looked back at me with an anxious expression as Ruthie tried to shove his big body out of the kitchen.

About an hour later, things had slowed down. Desserts had hit the floor, and several people had insisted I go out and greet a few people. As Anthony ushered me toward his table, I redirected and let him know I needed to go check on my parents first.

"Your parents are here?" he asked, a shadow crossing his face. "Your mom came?"

"Yes. She's fine. Really. Nothing to worry about. I'll be over right after."

"Can I come with you? I'd like to meet them."

With anyone else, I would have known exactly how I felt about that happening. Absolutely not something I wanted. But, with Anthony, as usual, I felt a little conflicted. I never knew how my mom was going to interact with people. Sometimes she could be fine – a regular mom. Sometimes a little light-hearted and even funny. Often, she was awkward. Her desire for attention had her interrupting people frequently and saying things that stopped the flow of conversation. That's what I was most used to. The worst was being on edge for when she went over a cliff – if she lashed out or said something cruel. It was rare for her to do something like that in public, but it's not like it had never happened.

That experience meant it was always my preference to not have people meet her. But Anthony was increasingly becoming an exception to my usual preferences. He already knew about my mom. Knew some of the worst things that she could do. I knew his desire to meet her wasn't because he was curious about the spectacle of my mother but, instead, because he wanted to support me and understand me more. It felt really nice to have that kind of steady support, so I nodded my head at him, indicating he could join me.

"Willow!" my mom stood as I approached, opening her arms for a hug. "Sweetie, your hair," she said as she tried to smooth out my disheveled locks. My usually straight hair couldn't quite survive the tangle it had been tied up in with the grease and sweat of the kitchen. I'd pulled it out of the bun and done my best to smooth through it before I left the kitchen, but it had been pretty hopeless.

"And your dress," she said, patting and pulling the neckline and shoulders. The apron had misshapen the top of my sweaterdress a bit, and my choices had been to either rock it the best I could or come out in a dirty apron.

"I think she looks beautiful – as she always does," Anthony said, taking a step closer to us.

"Oh, well," my mom said, stepping away from me and fully taking in the magnificence of Anthony Kaplan. She shifted her hand to smooth out her own hair as she said, "Of course, she does. She's a beautiful girl. And you are… ?"

"Hello, Mrs. Miller. I'm Anthony Kaplan. I'm Ruth Marsh's nephew." I was still between him and my mother, so he turned his attention to my dad who had stood up as well. Anthony put out his hand for my dad to shake and said, "Mr. Miller."

"Oh, how nice," my mom said. "You work with Ruth at the Co-op, right Willow?"

"Yes, Mom. She's the board president."

"Oh, that's nice."

The four of us looked at each other for a silent awkward moment until Anthony took the reins. "Willow has been responsible for this evening going off without a hitch. I would ask if you enjoyed your dinner, but I'm certain you did. And it's all thanks to your daughter."

"Anthony, that's ridiculous," I said. "I just helped out in the kitchen."

Anthony maintained his position that I was integral to the evening's success. I felt too tired to continue arguing, and I eventually stayed silent and watched Anthony working my parents. It didn't take long until they were agreeing with him about how smart and amazing I was. It was too much, and I didn't know why Anthony felt the need to press it so far, but I really just wanted to get to a table so I could take a big drink of water. I kept looking at my mom's glass on the table.

"I need to have Willow make the rounds a little more. There are some people sitting at my table that I should introduce her to. It was so nice to meet you."

My mom hugged me again, followed by my dad. As my dad released me, he asked, "Critter, are you okay? You look a little pale."

"I'm fine, Dad. Just a little tired. Enjoy your dessert. I'll see you both tomorrow, yeah? I'll stop by so we can take care of some things." My dad knew I meant so I could write out the checks for this month's bills. I always did it at their house and then showed them what they had left for the month.

"Critter?" Anthony asked as he began guiding me away from the table.

"Just a nickname from when I was little."

"It's cute. But I think I'll stick with Kitten. Grumpy little kitty cat."

The dining room was becoming an actual minefield for me. Before we got to Anthony's table where I could see his mother dressed even more elegantly than the night before, I heard a male voice say, "Anthony, hey, man."

Anthony stopped, and we saw that Chris was at a table with three other men. I nodded at all of them briefly. I knew they were Chris's regular crew – two of them had gone to school with me. None of them returned my small greeting.

"Chris," Anthony said, with a slight edge to his voice. It was obvious they were trying to snub me in front of him. He began to nudge me along again when we both heard Chris mutter, "She's a tease, man. Don't say I didn't warn you."

I felt every part of Anthony's body tense just behind me as he stopped walking. I heard the silence as he stopped breathing.

"Anthony, it's fine," I whispered.

"It damn well isn't fine," Anthony said in a voice loud enough to be heard by the entire table.

"Please, I just want to sit down for a minute." I pulled at his jacket sleeve and looked up at him. He looked down at me and then began ushering me toward his table again.

When we got there, I was greeted warmly by Ruthie and Dr. Marsh and icily by Anthony's mother.

Anthony pulled a chair out for me across from his mother, but he didn't sit with me as I'd expected. Instead, he said, "Be right back," and headed to Chris's table.

I watched him as he leaned over Chris's shoulder and issued some message meant for Chris and his friends. It was similar to watching him interact with Brendan. Instead of getting angry, the table of men looked contrite. They looked at Anthony like he had their complete attention and respect. To anyone else, Anthony looked like the in-charge businessman – the one I had faced at Ruthie's house all those weeks ago. But, to me, now that I knew him better, I could see it was just a veneer. His jaw was clenched, and his eyes were angry. And it was on my behalf.

"Willow? Willow?" I heard my name repeated a few times before I realized Ruthie was trying to get my attention. "Were you able to get anything to eat?"

"Oh, not yet. Maybe I could just have some water." I had a place setting in front of me with an empty glass. There were pitchers for water on the table, but I looked and saw all of them were empty.

"Anthony, there you are. Sit down this time," Mrs. Kaplan said as Anthony approached the chair next to mine. "Candice came all this way, and you've barely said three words to her."

I shifted my eyes from the empty pitcher to the gorgeous creature sitting next to Anthony's mother. Candice was the picture of what my mother wished I was. She and I shared a similar frame and hair color, but this woman made the most of everything God had given her. She wore a red wrap dress that hugged her long, slender frame, and I just knew she had on sky high heels under the table. Her hair was a thick glossy mane, and her makeup made her face look as perfect as a china doll's. She looked at Anthony like Sunshine eyeing a dish of cream.

Anthony sat down next to me and said, "Mother, you remember Willow. Willow this is my mother's friend, Candice Westerbrook."

"Your *mother's* friend?" Mrs. Kaplan exclaimed. "Oh, Anthony, you always have been such a silly boy."

I stifled a small grin at Anthony's mom calling him a boy.

"Are you one of the cooks?" Candice asked, looking at me. Her tone lifted distastefully on the word "cooks" and her expression twisted into one never before seen on a china doll.

"Willow is one of the volunteer organizers," Anthony said. "She's the reason this whole night came together."

"Oh, Anthony, don't be so modest. Ruth has told me everything you've been doing here. It seems to me you're trying to shift your own credit to someone else."

"Mother," Anthony said in an aggravated tone. "I've been dangling some connections I happen to have. Willow, on the other hand, has been planning, projecting, recruiting, training, and working – and she wasn't even supposed to be doing any of it. Aunt Ruth and I dragged her into it. Thank God we did because it really couldn't have happened without her."

Again, I was just too tired to argue. For whatever reason, Anthony wanted to sing my praises to everyone tonight. I wasn't feeling great, and I allowed myself to withdraw from the conversation in order to concentrate on staying upright at the table.

I wasn't sure how much time had passed. Anthony, his mother, and Candice had continued talking, but nothing registered with me until I heard Anthony say, "Actually, Willow and I are dating."

He put his arm around me as he said this, and I looked up at him in shock.

"And I think it's time to get her home. She's had a very long day."

He stood and began to pull my chair out for me.

I was completely confused and trying to rewind their conversation, which just sounded like static in my mind. I stood up from my chair, but I couldn't get my feet to work. My vision began to blur and everything around me was muted like I was underwater.

"Willow, are you okay?"

"Willow, what's wrong?"

"Willow, oh, no Willow!"

There were voices pulling me out of the fog I was in as the events of the last few hours played in my mind like a movie. I realized I was flat on my back on the floor of the Spruce Lake Dining Hall with a dozen voices murmuring above me. I could hear Anthony's voice was the nearest and could feel him holding my hand as he crouched next to me. I didn't want to open my eyes. I didn't want to face this moment, but what choice did I actually have? I counted down from ten in my mind and sat up quickly when I got to one.

"What's wrong with her?" I heard my mother say from the back of the circle of people crowded around me.

Anthony put his arm around my back and helped me

off the floor and into a chair. "She's fine," he said. "But she could use a little space."

The crowd began to move away, but Anthony remained. Dr. Marsh and my parents approached, and Anthony asked Dr. Marsh what in the hell was going on.

Dr. Marsh pulled a chair closer and sat across from me.

I heard Anthony say, "Emerson, for God's sake, turn up the music and get everyone to mind their own fucking business."

"Willow, what's going on honey?" Dr. Marsh asked me. "How are you feeling?"

"Tired," I said. "I'm just tired. I'm sorry about all this."

Dr. Marsh took my hand and put two fingers against my wrist to check my pulse.

"Could I have some water?" I asked once he was finished. "I'm sure I'll be fine. I just need a glass of water, and then I'll go home and rest."

Dr. March rubbed his thumbs under my eyes as he looked closely at my face. Then he took my hand, pulled some skin away from the top of it, and watched it after he released it.

"I agree with your diagnosis, Willow. Have you considered medical school?" He took the glass of water Anthony was holding out and gave it to me. "My question is - if you knew you were exhausted and dehydrated, why didn't you do something about it instead of making it worse, my dear? Drink up."

I took the glass and drank greedily.

Dehydrated. Huh. Did that really happen to people? I thought back to the last couple of days and realized I hadn't really eaten or had much to drink other than coffee. I knew I was running on empty, but that wasn't highly unusual.

I finished the glass and looked up at the small group of people around me. "Sorry," I said again.

My mother handed me a second glass and said, "So you two are dating?"

Chapter 12

I woke up, and, for a second, I thought the night before had been a dream. I stretched out on my bed in relief. And then I sat up like a shot. It most definitely hadn't been a dream.

Meeting Anthony's mom and the beautiful woman his mother clearly wanted him to marry while looking like a sweaty mess. Making a spectacle of myself by passing out in the middle of the dining hall. Having Anthony tell his mother we were dating.

Rewind.

What?

Why had he done that?

I remembered getting home after I'd recovered enough to be ushered out of the event. Anthony had insisted he drive me home. He kept telling everyone he would take care of it and that he would update my parents once I was settled. I had visions of his mother looking on with a horrified expression and my mother looking on with somewhat concerned but also very hopeful eyes. They all thought we were dating.

Again, why had he done that?

I looked around for Sunshine, but she wasn't in my room and, oddly, my door was closed. I needed to get up. Anthony had probably shut it before he left and poor Sunshine was probably frustrated.

What time was it?

I looked at my watch and saw it was after nine. I was relieved it was the weekend, or I would really be running late. I noticed a glass of water on the table next to my bed and smiled.

I was mortified at the events of last night, but I also felt grateful for the sweet way Anthony had taken care of everything. Taken care of me.

I reached over and drank every drop, feeling stupid that something as simple as a glass of water could have prevented all of this. That oversight was never happening again. No matter how busy I got.

Feeling much better, but still not great, I made myself get out of bed. I had on loose sweatpants and a tank top that I did not remember getting myself into. I touched my hand to my hair and remembered the disaster it had been the night before. I needed a shower.

Thinking I would have the energy for one after I had another cup of water, a counterproductive but necessary cup of coffee, and maybe some food, I opened the door and froze when I saw the scene in front of me.

Anthony sat on my couch with Sunshine on his lap. He looked relaxed in his running clothes with his laptop sitting open next to him.

"Hey, scruffy kitten," he said. His tone was teasing, but his eyes still showed concern. "Feeling better?"

"Anthony, what are you doing here?"

"What do you mean 'what am I doing here?'"

He scooted Sunshine off his lap onto the couch as he stood. He walked toward me while he asked, "Do you remember me bringing you home last night?" He looked at me, waiting a beat and then continued. "Come over here and sit down. Let me get you something to eat."

"No. I mean, yes. Yes, I remember you bringing me

home. Sort of."

"Willow, come sit down." He reached out for my hand.

I looked down at his and then back up to his face.

He gestured for me to come closer to him.

"Willow, are you okay? Come here." He walked the final step to me and grasped my hand, gently pulling me toward him. "Really, come sit down."

He guided me to the couch, and I sat in the spot he had been in. Sunshine jumped on my lap immediately to greet me. Anthony crouched in front of me and copied Dr. Marsh's actions from the night before. He put his hands on both sides of my face and stroked under my eyes.

"Anthony –"

"Hush," he said. He cradled one of my hands between his and gently pinched the skin and watched as it relaxed back into place.

"Anthony, I'm fine. I'm just confused about why you're still here."

"I'm here to take care of you."

The weight of that simple statement was substantial.

I took care of people. Not the other way around.

"I'm fine. I don't need any help."

"Do we need to revisit the events of last night? You were on the floor. Unresponsive. And then dazed until this morning… I think. At least I think you're not dazed anymore? You're arguing with me anyway, so that seems like a good sign. Like you're back to normal."

I couldn't help but laugh a little at his smirking face.

"You like arguing."

"With you, I do. Yes, you're right."

"Did you say what I think you said last night? Was that all part of my confusion? Did you tell everyone that we were… that we were… dating?"

"I did."

He didn't offer anything more. Just knelt in front me as if he hadn't said anything out of the ordinary.

"And why did you do that?"

"It's easier."

"Easier for what? For whom?"

"Everything. Everyone. Me with my mother and her hoping-to-be daughter-in-law Candice. For you and your mother. It just made everything stop. To say it – all the pressure just stops. You know?"

"Not really. It won't stop for me. My mother will start asking when the wedding will be as soon as she sees me again."

"We'll deflect. It'll be fine. Trust me. And when the time comes, you can be the one to break up with me. For whatever reason you want to make up that will satisfy your mother."

"This is crazy. What were you thinking?" I pulled at a lock of my hair in frustration and then remembered what a mess it was. What a mess I was. I started trying to get off the couch, but Anthony held me down.

"Willow, stop. You need to rest. I'm going to get you some breakfast."

I really wanted (and didn't want) a mirror. And a shower. A toothbrush. And for things to make sense again.

"I need a shower. Anthony, please let me up."

"Not yet," he said, putting pressure on my knees where his hands were gripping me. "You need to just sit here for a bit. At least two more cups of water before you get up this time."

"Why are you doing this? No one will believe we're dating! I mean, half the town has seen me arguing with you or frustrated with you or..."

"Enemies to lovers."

"Enemies to barely friends, you mean."

"Only because you didn't want to be friends," Anthony said, rising up from his kneeling position and moving his laptop so he could sit next to me. "It's perfect. You know, that's probably why I like you."

I looked at him in confusion. "Why you like me?"

"Yes. Because you don't like me at all. That makes everything easier. And better."

"That's not true!"

"What's not true? That it's better? Or that you don't like me?"

"Both?"

"Well, you didn't like me. Not for a long time. And you actually hate my money."

"That's true. I do hate your money."

"I love that. It helps me know you're not after anything. That we can actually be friends and that if we pretend to be in a relationship, you aren't doing it for the usual reasons – money or status or…"

"Why would I care about that?"

"Exactly! If you do it, it's because we find it mutually beneficial. And I think with our mothers, that might be the case. Besides, I like spending time with you, and this means I get to. Win/win."

"I have to think about this. Honestly, I think it will make things worse with my mom instead of better. In the long run."

"I'll smooth the way. I'll help you figure it out with her somehow. I promise. That will be my mission while we do this."

"Why can't you just tell your mom that you don't want to date Candice?"

"If it isn't Candice, it will be someone else. Or just constant questions about why I'm still up here. Since my father died, she's fixated on organizing my life."

"You're like – like old for that!"

"Did you just call me old? Did you?"

"Well, yeah. I mean, she also called you a boy recently."

"It's all new. Trust me. She never paid me any

attention when I actually was a boy."

Well, that was tragic.

Anthony continued, "She's just bored now that she can't organize my father and now that she has fewer social events to be a part of. She wants me to get married and get back to doing important work (her version of important) so she can tag along. That's all this is."

"Well, she won't get that if you're dating me. *Fake* dating me."

"Exactly."

I leaned my head back against the couch and looked at the ceiling. What did it matter if I agreed to this? It was basically my version of the perfect relationship. Hanging out with someone I liked and found attractive but where both of us knew there wasn't any future in it. The only difference was no sex. I could live with that, right? I was going to be living with no sex anyway at the rate I was going.

"What's going on in that mind of yours?" Anthony asked, reaching over to stroke Sunshine's front paw.

"I'm thinking about how it's the perfect relationship for me. How all I ever want is to find someone who I can spend some time with but where there are no strings. No expectations. No future. So, I guess, why not?"

"Perfect! Except as your fake boyfriend, we're going to talk soon about your future goals. That bar seems pretty low to me."

∞∞∞

An hour or so later, I was finishing a pancake breakfast Anthony had made. I had showered, which had been heaven and come back out to my kitchen table set with coffee, pancakes, fruit, and maple syrup.

"Feeling better?" Anthony had topped off my coffee cup but kept nudging my glass of water closer.

"A million times better. Thank you for everything. Last night and today. It was really stupid of me."

"Selfless of you. That's what you said, right?"

"Being stupid enough to become dehydrated for no reason? That's selfless?"

I looked at Anthony's open expression. He almost always had that expression when he was with me now. He seemed determined to praise me. To notice things about me. Was this what friendship really was? Being there for each other in a different way – a really special way?

"The reason is that you were running around taking care of everyone else and not yourself," Anthony said. "That's selfless. But we aren't going to argue about it because I know we won't agree. And I have something else I want to argue with you about anyway." His eyes lit with amusement.

"Oh, really?" I asked. "And what is it you *want* to argue with me about?"

"You're not going to like it. Maybe drink some more water first."

I felt dread in the pit of my stomach. I racked my brain trying to imagine what he was thinking about. *Was he leaving soon?* No, that didn't make sense. Why would we argue about that? But I hated the thought, which was unusual and scary. I usually chose unemotional and uninvested for a reason.

"Your photography, Willow."

He had intentionally delivered this news when I wasn't looking at him, and I froze with my gaze still fixed to my coffee cup. My first feeling was anger. I wanted to scream, "How dare you?" as I pushed him out the door. But – (a) I couldn't move his big body no matter how hard I tried and (b) what good would it do? He knew. He *knew*!

"Willow," he said in a low voice. "Why is this a secret?"

"Why were you snooping in my house?" I raised my eyes to his for a brief moment but quickly looked away and stood from the table. I was embarrassed. I knew I shouldn't be, but it was just so private. I felt ridiculously exposed.

"I wasn't snooping. I was looking. I didn't know where anything was when we got here last night. I was trying to get you into bed and take care of Sunshine. It's not like there was a sign on the door that said, 'Keep out.'"

I stomped out of the kitchen, but Anthony was up quickly and followed right behind me.

"Leave me alone, Anthony." I froze, realizing I couldn't get away from this. It didn't matter where I went. He was still going to know.

"Willow." He reached out and lightly gripped the back of my elbow. "Willow, come on. Let's just talk about it. I just want to understand."

"Can we just not talk about it, please?" I asked, finally turning to face him. I took a deep breath and looked up into his eyes. He looked concerned, which surprised me. I guess I expected him to be sort of laughing about it. Ready to make fun of me. To mock me.

"Willow, why are you afraid of me knowing? You know I'm a fan of your work. I think it's incredible. I also feel like a bit of an idiot for some of the comments I made in the past – made me a little mad that you had kept it a secret when I stumbled upon it last night. But then I had to admit the comments I made when we met at Aunt Ruth's were all my own fault.

"And now, what I'm about to say is going to sound bad because of things I've said before. Assumptions I've made before about your work at the Co-op. Which I should never have done."

I wanted to evaporate. Just sort of disappear into thin air. I did not want to have this conversation.

I guess my feelings were evident on my face because

Anthony's eyes darted from my eyes to my mouth and back up to my eyes and said, "Fine. Fine. You win. We won't talk about it now, but I don't understand why not."

"And you won't tell Ruthie? Or anyone else? Don't tell my parents!"

"Of course, I won't, Willow. Not if you don't want me to. I just wanted to understand."

Chapter 13

"Mom, please don't get too excited about this. We just started dating. He doesn't even really live here. It's casual."

"Willow Miller," my mother said, putting her hands firmly on her hips as she scolded me. "You have to change your attitude. You have to be open. Optimistic. Ready."

"Well, I'm not really any of those things, Mom. So there's your answer. It's not going where you want it to go. Just please, can we drop this?"

"No, we cannot. You are going to invite that man over for dinner. Your father and I want to get to know him better. He seems like such a nice man. And so handsome!"

I found it interesting that, although I didn't want

Anthony to come to my parents' house for dinner, it wasn't for the usual reasons. Usually, I had so much anxiety about what my mother might do, but Anthony knew all that. And Anthony was the kind of man who wouldn't be phased if my mother lashed out at him. It wouldn't penetrate his strong will. No, my resistance wasn't that. It was knowing how high my mom's hopes were getting. Knowing that the more she got to know Anthony, the higher they would climb. She thought this was my moment – the one like she had with my dad. She had thought the whole humiliation of passing out at the dinner was incredibly romantic. Romantic! I had been walking around the Co-op since with a burning blush staining my face.

"Critter, we'd like to get to know the man," my dad said as he walked into the kitchen where my mom and I were having coffee.

"Dad! You too?" I couldn't believe it. He had never shown any interest in anyone I'd dated.

"Yes, Critter. Anthony seems like a good one."

"He is. But it's casual. It's just –"

"I can make my beef stroganoff," my mom said,

noting another of her nine by thirteen casseroles.

∞∞∞

"Ruthie, not you, too."

"Of course, I'm happy about this," Ruthie said. We were sitting in the Co-op café after reviewing some quarterly reports. "I couldn't be happier. Two of my favorite people together! I'm thrilled. I want you both to come over on Sunday. It's supposed to be sunny, and it will be nice to spend some time out on the lake before it gets too cold. We can go out on the boat. Loren and I haven't had a chance to do it all year."

"Ruthie, really, that sounds more like a family thing –"

"Oh, it will be a family thing all right. That woman – Anthony's mother – has decided to stick around and she'll have to be invited. It's one reason I want to get together so soon. I need a buffer, and you and Anthony will be the perfect distraction."

"But, Ruthie, we're not so much dating, dating. Like it's not something serious. We just –"

"Just what?" she asked, giving me a concerned look. "Willow, Anthony isn't one of your love 'em and leave 'em types. He doesn't deserve that."

I knew Ruthie liked me. I did. But Anthony was her beloved nephew. If she thought I was going to hurt him... I hated lying to her, and I didn't think her care for me would fully survive once the fake breakup happened. She would have to take his side. My heart hurt thinking that this idea was putting my relationship with Ruthie in jeopardy.

"Just nothing," I said.

"Willow! Mrs. Marsh!" Emerson made her way over to our table. "I'm so happy to have found you both at the same time!"

Emerson was soft-spoken, as she always was, but her excitement was evident as she continued.

"I was so happy with the way the dinner turned out. I know we already have more work to do to gear up for the locavore event, but I was hoping to have a small get-together to thank the people who worked so hard to make all this happen. We're really headed in the right direction, and the two of you with Anthony are the reason why. Please say you'll come! Next Wednesday night. It's a bonfire on the lake. Have Anthony bring his guitar. Tell him I insist!"

While Ruthie and Emerson talked about the plans for the bonfire, I sent Anthony a text message. "You said this made all the pressure stop! I've never felt so much pressure in my life. We have three dates forced upon us in the next few days."

"Four," Anthony quickly texted back. "My mother wants to have dinner tonight, and I was really hoping you would join us."

∞∞∞

"I can't believe you're making me do this. She hates me and won't want me here. How is this helping?" I grumbled to Anthony as he guided me to the table where I knew his mother was already waiting.

Anthony had told me to meet him at one of the more upscale restaurants in town. I had never been to it before, but the chef sometimes came into the Co-op.

"She'll be nice. I promise," Anthony said.

"You talked to her about this? You had to what? Convince her to be nice to me?"

"Willow, please. She will be nice, or we'll leave. I could really use a friend tonight. It's painful being with her by myself. And I wouldn't do it at all, but I feel sorry for her. The sooner I convince her I'm not going to provide her with society entertainment anytime soon, the sooner she'll leave. Just help me get through this. Please?"

Not for the first time, I thought about what Anthony's childhood must have been like and softened. I couldn't say my childhood had been easy, but I couldn't imagine having parents who sent me away like his had.

"Fine. Let's just get this over with."

"Anthony, darling. And your little friend. Hello." Anthony's mother straightened her silverware as she greeted us. "So nice of you to join us. Such a quaint little place," she said, in a tone that expressed her value for our community's version of upscale.

I jolted a little when I felt Anthony's hand settle firmly on my lower back. He guided me to my chair and then helped push me toward the table before sitting down himself.

"I was devastated Candice had to leave so soon," Mrs. Kaplan began saying.

"Mother," Anthony said in a warning tone.

"Well, she'll see you in the city when you come back. And when will that be again? Exactly? Will you be there for the Cohen Gala? I'm sure they'll send an invitation."

"No, Mother. I'm not returning to New York anytime soon. You know my home base is Boston anyway."

"Yes, but now that your father's gone – I need you, Anthony! You need to come take your place in the city. I was so upset when you decided to sell the company, but now I see the benefit. You will have all the time for more *important* things. I see it now."

"Mother, the Cohen Gala is not an 'important thing' for me."

"Well, it is for me!" Mrs. Kaplan's high-pitched whine rang out in our corner of the restaurant. "You owe it to me, Anthony, as your mother. You can't leave me to… to *rot* by myself." She lowered her voice and turned away from me a bit. She talked as if I somehow couldn't hear her just because she had indicated she didn't want me to. "No one will invite me to the Gala, Anthony. Not if you aren't going."

"I'm sorry about that, Mother. Really, I am." Anthony put his hand over mine and began to caress it. "But I'm happy here, and I'm not leaving anytime soon."

Mrs. Kaplan looked at Anthony's small public display of affection in disdain. I hadn't understood until this moment why Anthony had made his proclamation about us dating. This woman was relentless. Anthony clearly had the will to stand up to her, but it had to be so wearing. To have a mother who only wanted a relationship to get what she could from it. To show zero love to her son. Ever. My mother's issues made life hard, and I carried my own share of hurt from things she had said to me. And things she had done. But I never doubted that she loved me.

Impulsively, I wrapped my other hand around Anthony's and leaned into him as much as I could from my seat. "I'm sorry, Mrs. Kaplan. We just can't seem to spend any time apart at the moment. That's how it is when you care about someone, you know? And I think we can agree I'm not right for any galas or city life, so we're better off staying here for now."

She muttered something about gold diggers under her breath, but since we were all literally right next to each other, it was clear what she had said. Then more loudly, she stated, "Some people will pretend all kinds of things to get what they're after. Anthony, please see this for what it is." Unlike my mother's face when she was cruel, Mrs. Kaplan's face gave nothing away. The Botox was effective.

"Mother, this is your first and *only* warning. If you want me to spend time with you, you will be civil to Willow. No slip-ups. No exceptions."

"It's fine, Anthony. Mrs. Kaplan, I think you might want to look again if you think anyone would have to *pretend* to care about your son." I meant it even though I knew the irony of our situation made the statement ridiculous. I wanted to somehow make sure Anthony understood that I meant it as well. Even though we weren't for real, I hated that his mother might have any ability to make him doubt that someone would really love him for himself.

"What are you going to have, Puppy?" I asked, drawing on the only pet name that I felt I could actually call him. He was still generally the open, eager Golden Retriever I had once accused him of being.

"*Puppy*?" Anthony mouthed to me as his mother gave up for the moment and buried her face in her menu.

I grinned.

"Well, *Kitten*," he began, "you know how much I love getting a glimpse of your preferences, so I'm going to have whatever you're having."

∞∞∞

"You wouldn't dare!" I squealed as Anthony held me suspended over the water. We were out on Ruthie's boat, and Anthony was threatening to drop me into the lake. It was too cold, so I knew he couldn't be serious. I hoped he wasn't serious? But, just in case he was, I was trying to figure out how to make sure I took him with me if I did go in.

"Anthony Kaplan, leave the girl alone," Ruthie scolded from her spot next to Dr. Marsh. Being on their boat was like being in another world. To have grown up in a lake community, I hadn't spent very much time at all on the water. A few kayak outings, but that was really it. This was luxury. Ruthie and Dr. Marsh sat in the seats by the steering wheel. Anthony and I were sitting on the benches at the front of the boat. I felt a weird conflict at how much fun I was having.

These were the light-hearted days of the people who had money. The lake was shimmering. The vibrant fall leaves were beautifully reflecting on the surface. The chicken salad sandwiches Ruthie had packed tasted better than any chicken salad sandwich I'd ever had. And, best of all, Anthony's mom had gone back to New York – at least temporarily. She had been invited to something she *couldn't miss* but had warned she would be back. The experience was thrilling, and somehow that made me feel guilty. Ashamed. Most people didn't get this, and I didn't want to like it. It wasn't fair to like it. To accept that it felt good.

Anthony was entertaining us all, and we weren't even having to pretend. Even though we were perpetuating the lie about dating, we could be ourselves – friends – and it was enough. Ruthie didn't need us to prove that we liked each other. For the moment at least, she was on our side. Our collective side. I still didn't want to think about what would happen when it was time for the fake break-up.

I suppose my parents were on our side, too, but that was still kind of a hard sell. The dinner a few nights ago had been fine. Anthony had made it fine. I'd been a little embarrassed for him to come to my parents' small home and be served a dinner in my mom's fashion – especially after what I'd experienced for lunch at Ruthie's and at dinner with his mother. My parents' house and my mom's nine by twelve casseroles and chipped plates were as far from that as a person could get.

But it had been fine. Anthony had come in and charmed the pants off both my mom and my dad. He'd found some common ground talking about tools with my dad, and my mom had been on her best behavior. Anthony, it seemed, could be comfortable anywhere and could put anyone at ease. He actually brought out the best in my parents, and it was a relief to have that kind of time with them all.

Anthony had listened to his Aunt Ruth and had

stopped dangling me over the boat, but, even though pretending wasn't necessary, he pulled me to him once he sat us firmly back on the bench again. The sun was starting to consider setting, and Anthony settled me into his side with his arm gripping me, urging me to watch the sky with him. I felt little sparks in all the places our bodies were touching - up and down my side connected with his, our bare legs shifting against each other, my arm where his firm, warm hand grasped me.

"Anthony," I said, my words muffled from where my face was now burrowed into his neck.

"Yes, Kitten?"

"Stop," I laughed as I nudged him in mock frustration. "You don't have to do that. No one can hear."

"Hey, I was calling you Kitten before any of this started."

"Oof. Fine. *Puppy*." I reminded myself it didn't matter how romantic it felt to be cradled up to him, teasing each other while we watched the sunset. This wasn't real, and, while I was happy to run interference with his mom, this charade was probably only going to make things difficult for me with Ruthie and my parents the longer it went on.

"Look," I began. "I know you said this... this thing about us dating in the heat of the moment the other night. And I get why you did it. Your mother... Well, she's just awful, Anthony. I'm sorry to say it, but she's terrible to you. I'll pretend with you all day long to keep her from giving you a hard time."

I pulled away from Anthony's chest just enough to be able to see his face. He let out a heavy sigh and said, "But I'm actually making things harder for you."

"No, not exactly," I hedged. "Well, yeah, I guess that's what I'm saying."

I separated myself from him a bit more. "I know you didn't mean to. And it's not a big deal. Truly. We can still fix it. I just think we should do it soon. My parents think this is it for me. It doesn't matter how many times I've told them I'm not the marrying kind. And Ruthie – she has this warped perception that I'm a heartbreaker, and she will be furious with me if she thinks I did that to you. Even if it's completely made up, and no one else would ever believe that I could actually break your heart."

"Wait a minute," Anthony said, turning to face me while giving more of his back to Ruthie and Dr. Marsh. "That's a lot of information you just spilled. More than you usually do. First, why wouldn't anyone believe you could break my heart? What the hell does that mean?"

I glared at him. "You know what that means."

"Enlighten me."

"Why would you make me say that out loud?"

Anthony just stared at me, urging me to continue.

"Fine – you know you're ridiculously out of my league. Only people who love me like my parents and Ruthie do can accept this *relationship* without questioning it. Everyone else clearly thinks it's crazy. Case in point: your mother's reaction. There's no way they are going to believe that not only did you date me, but that I called it off. I think we just need to tell them the truth – that we made it up to save you some grief with your mother."

"Wait just a damn minute. Any man would be lucky to date you, Willow, and everyone knows that. You're beautiful and smart and funny. And – "

"Stop!" I was squirming in my seat, so uncomfortable that he thought I was asking him to build up my confidence. "Stop! I think I'm fine. Stop doing that! I'm happy with myself, but it's just a fact. We are from two different worlds, and I don't belong in yours."

"Well, I completely disagree. And, as for the rest... What's this about never marrying and being a heartbreaker? I remember Aunt Ruth talking like Chris was one in a long line of men. But I can't quite see that after getting to know you."

"Because it isn't true!" I could feel my cheeks burning. "I've seriously dated two men before Chris. That's it. Ruthie and my parents want me to settle down. They don't... they don't like my way of thinking about long-term relationships."

"Which is...?"

"Well, I do want a relationship. But I know it won't look like relationships usually do. I know it won't advance past a certain point."

"You mean physically?" Confusion crossed Anthony's face. "Of course, you don't mean that. Your parents and Ruthie have nothing to do with that." Anthony's eyes moved as if he were adding up sums in his head – trying to assess all the variables. He finally gave up and said, "What is it then? What do you mean it won't advance past a certain point?"

"Ugh. Anthony, this stuff doesn't matter. It's just… It's just how I am. I don't do feelings. I mean, of course, I do feelings. I have to like a person to want to be in a relationship. I just know it's not going to turn into hearts and flowers and love. Marriage and babies. That's just not me."

I waited for Anthony to argue with me as everyone always did about this topic. But he just settled in a bit more and redirected his gaze to the sunset again.

After a little while, he said, "So because I'm *out of your league* and because you want a relationship but a casual one, we need to tell your parents and Ruthie – and basically everyone except my mother – that we aren't dating. That we made it up."

"Yes, I think that would be best," I said, looking over at Ruthie and Dr. Marsh to make sure they were still preoccupied with each other. They were. It was pretty sweet.

"Well," Anthony said, pulling me into him again, "I have a different idea."

"You do?"

"Yes. I propose we have a relationship on your terms. I happen to really like those terms myself."

Chapter 14

Sunshine looked at me as if to ask, "Are you going to change clothes again?" I gave her a quick pat on the head and said, "I'm done, okay? Give me a break!"

I was incredibly nervous. After Anthony's proposal about a casual relationship, we hadn't really talked. I mean we'd talked, but we'd been avoiding the topic. Well, I'd been avoiding the topic. I think Anthony was just giving me space to consider. And, clearly, I was considering since I hadn't pressed him about telling Ruthie the truth. We'd ended the day on the boat perpetuating the charade. And, apart from my chaotic mind, it had been lovely. Anthony cuddling me on the boat, holding my hand, teasing me in the sweetest way while giving me that twinkly-eyed look he seemed to save just for me. Who wouldn't consider continuing that? But it was making me crazy. I knew it was a bad idea. He was the best friend I had ever had. I didn't know how to navigate that kind of friendship, so I didn't know if that kind of connection fizzled over time anyway, or if I would be risking one of the best things that had ever happened to me by doing my casual relationship thing.

Sunshine looked at me with accusing eyes as I pulled the sweater off and rummaged in my closet again. Standing in jeans and a bra, I heard a text coming in on my phone. Fairly sure it was Anthony since we now had a pretty regular texting connection, I was embarrassed in front of myself about how quickly I leapt to get the phone from my bed.

Anthony: I'm picking you up. I'll be there in 10.

Me (panicked): No! We're meeting there. I'm not ready.

Anthony: Well, get ready. Time's ticking.

I threw my phone back on my bed and grabbed the discarded sweater again. Within a half hour, we were pulling up to Spruce Lake for Emerson's bonfire.

"So, I don't want to push you," Anthony said as he

turned the car off. "But do you want to talk about things – about us – before we're on display in front of everyone tonight?"

I'd been getting ready to open the car door, but I let my hand drop back into my lap.

"Anthony, I... I have been thinking a lot about it. Obviously. First, I know it's pathetic, but I have to make sure you're serious. I know you don't want to hear the whole *out of your league* thing, but I really don't see you wanting to date me. I don't feel like I could possibly be your type."

Anthony scoffed. "Willow, you're every man's type as far as I can tell. Unless that man is an idiot like that Chris guy."

I smiled and gave a little huff. "He's not an idiot. I mean, it turns out he is an idiot, but that isn't why things ended. They ended for all the regular reasons when it comes to me and relationships. And that's the other part I've been worried about. I do want to be in a relationship on my terms. I really, really do. And you are the dream for that. I love spending time with you. And obviously I find you attractive." I murmured the last part, embarrassed.

"Obviously," Anthony said with a proud and teasing smile.

"But we just figured out how to be friends. In my experience, if the relationship has a boundary about how far it can go, it eventually ends, and any friendship goes with it. I don't want that to happen with us. Your friendship is... important to me." I could feel my eyes tearing up in an unusual rush of emotion.

"Ah, Kitten," Anthony said, reaching for my hand. "Your friendship is important to me, too. Very important. But I know how to do friends with benefits. It's all I've ever really done. I still consider my exes to be friends."

I closed my eyes to think, but instead felt myself focusing on the feeling of Anthony's hand caressing mine.

"Willow?"

"Yeah," I said. "I'm just thinking."

"Can I present some additional arguments in favor of my position while you're thinking?"

I could imagine his blue eyes full of mischief as he

said this. "Sure. Try your best."

Anthony didn't say anything at all. Instead, I heard him shift in his seat toward me, and he began to rub his finger up the inside of my forearm. Tingles followed the line he made up to my elbow. He cradled my hand with his and brought it toward him.

Like a Victorian-era virgin, I actually gasped when he brought my hand to his lips. I sighed as he kissed my fingers, the inside of my wrist. It was just *so* good. Touch was important to me, but this touch – *his* touch felt heightened. Extra.

"Anthony… " I said, feeling so much conflict. He needed to stop, but I didn't want him to ever stop.

"I'm not finished with my arguments," he whispered, and he brought a hand up to my cheek and turned my face toward him.

I didn't want to face reality, which is why I still had my eyes tightly shut, but I needed to see his face. I reluctantly opened them and locked my gaze on his icy blue eyes. So clear and so open. I saw his mouth hitch in a small grin as he moved his other hand up so he was cradling my face.

"Anthony, I'm not sure this is a good idea," I whispered the words even as I felt myself leaning toward him.

"Shh," he coaxed. "I'm not finished with my arguments." He leaned closer, stroking the side of my mouth with his thumb, until his lips touched mine. Softly and sweetly. My mind felt the sweetness, but my body was rioting. Sparks of energy were firing throughout every part of me until it felt like I would burn from the inside out. I leaned in for another kiss and felt Anthony's fingers grip behind my ears into my hair. We nipped at each other, and I felt my heart racing. Before Anthony could take the kiss deeper, I pulled back to look at him again. There was no triumph in his eyes. No sign he was toying with me.

I leaned my forehead against his shoulder and whispered, "Please don't hate me when this is over."

∞∞∞

Emerson's bonfire was… romantic. Not exactly what

I needed when I was trying to figure out the boundaries of my relationship with Anthony. She'd put a spread of snacks and drinks on the porch of the dining hall, but the main event was the bonfire that was being lit as Anthony and I approached the lake.

Emerson's co-workers who had helped serve the dinner were all there. She'd also invited the camp board members and some donors, and I saw Ruthie and Dr. Marsh talking to that circle of guests.

"Willow! Anthony!" she greeted when she saw us. "I'm so glad you made it. And you brought your guitar, Anthony! Thank you so much!"

Anthony lifted the shoulder of the arm that was carrying his guitar case in a half shrug. "I'm not sure you'll be so excited when you hear me play. Honestly, Emerson, I just mess around. Your lot should be the ones playing tonight."

"Oh, no," she said, dismissively. "Classical musicians are the worst for something like this. We'd all fuss about our instruments and feel like we needed sheet music and a plan. Someone who *messes around* on a guitar is exactly what we need tonight!"

"Well, don't say I didn't warn you."

Anthony typically didn't lack confidence in his abilities, so it was strange to hear him express concern about his playing. And it was even stranger to connect that lack of confidence to the emotional and skilled way he actually played once we were gathered around the fire.

He played some fingerstyle songs – some Mark Knopfler, some John Mayer, and honestly some things I just didn't recognize. They had everyone swaying along and chatting softly to each other and had me in a sort of blissed-out state. His playing was full of tension, longing, feeling - and when Emerson and others had complimented him on his playing, he thanked them but again downplayed it as something he messed around with – mostly when he was growing up and away at school. The rich notes ringing in the night hit me particularly profoundly after I heard him say that. It broke my heart a little to imagine a pre-teen Anthony self-soothing with this emotional music when he was growing up and had no family or support around him.

After a while, he insisted someone else among the

group of musicians must play some guitar. One of Emerson's co-workers finally relented and took the instrument from Anthony. She was more of a play-along guitarist, and Emerson had been right about her musician group. The guitarist had to start two or three times once they decided to do a sing along of an Adele song. They had to keep stopping to discuss what key they wanted to sing in, and the guitarist would try again until they found a key they could all agree on.

Anthony asked if I wanted to take a walk while they were singing. Ruthie and Dr. Marsh had already left, and Anthony led me down closer to the lake where we walked along the water.

"It's beautiful here," he said, taking my hand in his. We could hear the singing and laughter fading as we walked farther away.

"Totally beautiful. I wonder if the kids know how lucky they are when they come in the summer." I breathed in the night air and appreciated the sound of the lake lapping the shore.

"Well, that probably depends."

I waited for Anthony to continue.

"It probably depends on whether they want to be here or not. Sometimes the kid doesn't get to choose."

His words hit my heart like little stabs. "Was it awful?" I asked. "When you were sent away to school?"

"It wasn't awful all the time, no. But sometimes it could be awful, I guess. I think you learn some bad habits if you don't feel like you have someone on your side when you're a kid. But you also learn some good ones. It's all a trade-off." He squeezed my hand as if to say it was no big deal.

"Well, I've met your mom. I think I have an idea of who she is. But what about your dad? I mean he was Ruthie's brother, right?"

"Yes, he was Aunt Ruth's brother, but he was quite a bit younger. They didn't completely grow up together, although I think Aunt Ruth tried to connect with him as much as she could." Anthony steered me back up onto the grounds but in a rambling pathway that would eventually get us back to the bonfire. "I think he tried his best, but he had one focus: money. He was single-minded in his desire to grow the business and for me to one day take it over and continue to grow it. He had some advantages growing up but not early on. My grandparents were immigrants just after they married and struggled for most of their lives in the US. Things started to improve by the time my father was finishing high school, but he knew what hardship was, and he wanted no part of it."

"Help me connect the dots," I said, leaning into him a bit. "Where did they immigrate from? And the religion thing? It's so important for Ruthie but not for you or your family?"

"I don't know a lot of the history – the why's or when's. That's what happens, I guess, when you spend your childhood with other kids instead of family. What I do know is that my grandparents were refugees from Ukraine. My grandfather knew about building and worked construction most of his life after they landed here. Aunt Ruth was very close to them, and I know their religion was an important part of their lives. And then she married Loren who had a similar background – minus the hardship. They became this Jewish power couple, you know? But my father, I think he just didn't care. Thinking about how he ended up with someone like my mother and things I saw growing up… Status mattered to him. What other people thought mattered to him. He was determined to break the mold he was born into and did it at the expense of connection and relationships. Aunt Ruth broke the mold but kept all of that."

Anthony guided me toward the door of one of the practice huts we were passing. "Enough of my past," he said. "Let's pound on a piano in the middle of the woods. How often does a person get to do that?"

I stepped into the hut and stupidly felt around for a light switch. "I guess no electricity, huh?"

"I think these are daytime, acoustic huts. Come here," he said, pulling me toward the piano bench. He turned on his phone flashlight and put it on the top of the piano. It illuminated the small hut like a little lantern.

"I only know that one song on the piano – the one that two people play? We used to play it at school. Do you know it?" I asked Anthony as we both positioned ourselves in front of the instrument.

He started the rhythm chords and smiled at me expectantly.

I tested out a few notes on my end and then tried to correctly time the entrance of my melody line with his rhythm line. It was silly and fun. And, honestly, a little ridiculous. We did what kids do with the song and kept starting over, speeding up each time until we were laughing so hard we couldn't play anymore. Anthony was right – it was strange to play the piano in the middle of the woods.

Finally regaining my breath after a solid bout of laughing, I stood and asked, "Should we get back?"

Anthony spun around on the bench away from the piano. He pulled me toward him between his open legs and laced his fingers with mine. It felt natural, as everything had tonight. But I still heard alarm bells ringing. "Anthony, are you sure this is smart?"

"Totally sure." He stood up and walked me a few steps until my back hit the wall near the door. "I've wanted to do this since the first moment I saw you."

"Now that, my *friend*, is a lie. Or a line. Or both. I think it also means you don't remember the first time you saw me."

"I absolutely remember the first time I saw you," he

said, tracing patterns along the side of my neck. "You were the cute, grouchy cashier at the Co-op. Friendly to everyone but me. It was fascinating and annoying. And attractive."

"You thought it was attractive that I was grouchy and rude to you?"

"I thought it was curious. And I thought you were stunning."

"Anthony, I am standing with you in a dark hut in the woods with your arms around me. You don't have to lay it on so thick."

"I'm just telling you the truth. You were stunning, and I thought you would be a fun distraction while I was here in Maine. I thought maybe we could… You know."

"Benefits, no friends?"

"Something like that." He kept tracing little circles and lines on my neck with one hand and slipped the other one just under my sweater and copied the movements along my waist. "But then the more I saw of you, the more I just liked you. And the friends part was more important."

"So maybe we should keep it there?" I asked, a little short of breath.

"Nope. This is better," he said. "I promise we'll be fine."

He leaned down and kissed me. This kiss was not sweet like the one in his SUV. This one burned hot from the beginning, and I couldn't resist the intensity. I gripped his sweater with both hands and kissed him back with everything I had.

"So good, Willow."

I nodded as I returned his kisses eagerly. "Anthony," I said in between delicious kisses. "We have to get back." I was loving it but also panicking at how much I was feeling. At how much I didn't want this to stop. "They know where we are because of the piano playing," I tried again.

"Are you afraid we'll be busted by the camp counselors?" I could feel him grin as he kissed up the column of my neck.

I laughed a little. "No, but… It's a lot. I'm feeling a lot right now."

He pulled back and looked at me. "Okay, Kitten.

We'll go slow." He leaned down and kissed me softly again before guiding me back into the night toward the bonfire.

Chapter 15

"We're going to get outvoted this time," Ruthie said in a worried voice. "I don't think we can stop it."

We were huddled together in my small office because she'd told me we needed some privacy for this conversation.

"That Bill Davis is going to get the votes and he'll take my place as president. When that happens, I don't think we can stop the direction he's been pushing for the last few years."

"But what about Lee and Sharon? Won't they stick with us?"

"Lee is checked out, and Sharon's husband has been getting cozy with Bill. I think he's wormed his way in with her, and she'll vote him in."

This was disturbing news that I didn't really want to

face. Ruthie had been leading the direction of the Co-op for as long as I'd been involved. We had a duty to both our suppliers and our member owners. It was a careful balance, and we worked hard to strike the right one. We didn't always get it right, but we were always working toward that goal.

Bill Davis, on the other hand, was a businessman who didn't really care about our owners or suppliers. He cared about success. He'd come to town about ten years ago and had opened an exclusive boutique golf resort just outside our town. It wasn't one of the big ones a pro golfer would visit. It was the kind people with money would go for a holiday. I had to admit, he'd built something beautiful, and it was a success and provided a boost for the entire town. But that kind of business wasn't the kind of business the Co-op was. That kind of business didn't have a lot of balance to it. It was just about the bottom line. The member owners had voted him on to the board because he was a successful businessman, but they wouldn't like his message if he was leading. Unfortunately, it wasn't the member owners who voted to fill the officer roles. It was just the board members. The bottom line was the message Bill Davis had been preaching since the moment he attended his first meeting. The Co-op should have a bigger bottom line. In our environment, that meant carrying predominantly exclusive, specialty products. That was the avenue to Bill seeing more money running through the Co-op. Never mind if it hurt the farmers and employees or ran the risk of either total failure of the business or, at best, turning it into a place where only people with a bank account of a certain size could shop. Although we had our fair share of tourists shopping in our store, most of the year our business was from locals and restaurant owners who had their own challenges but made the hard decision to buy local food at a premium instead of getting their produce and meat from a conglomerate that would deliver in their big, refrigerated trucks. Many of them couldn't continue if we substantially increased our prices.

"Surely, we can get people to come around. You've always been able to before." I looked at Ruthie hopefully. She wasn't one to give up – not that I'd ever seen, but she didn't seem to think there was a battle left to fight.

"This place is important to me. You know that, Willow. I'll be heart-broken if we go Bill Davis's direction. But, more than that, I'm worried for you."

She reached over and took both my hands. I adored Ruthie, but this was odd behavior and it forced me to really look at her. Her expression had me worried.

"Loren has told me I need to step down entirely from the board if they elect Bill." She squeezed my hands as she looked at me and continued. "I've been having some health problems –"

My gasp was audible, but Ruthie quickly continued. "It's nothing to worry about. I just need to keep my stress levels down. Doctor's orders," she said with a small grin. "Loren knows where my blood pressure will go if I have to be a part of Bill's plans. But I don't want to leave you on your own to fight him."

"Ruthie," I said, stunned. "How can… What can I do to help? I'm so sorry – of course, you have to step down! You need to do that now. Don't wait for the election. You have to take care of yourself. Dr. Marsh is right!"

"I don't want to let you down, Willow. I don't want to

leave you on your own."

"I'm fine. Really. I can hear your voice and advice in my head anytime I need it." I lied through my teeth. I could hear her voice and her advice, but I wasn't fine. I didn't like Bill Davis's direction any more than she did, and I did not want to do this without her. She brought a force to the table that I would never have. A presence.

"I wish it didn't have to be this way. I'm so sorry."

∞∞∞

"Want to sneak off to the hut later?" Anthony's text came in later that afternoon.

Since that day in the hut, we'd been like teenagers – making out anywhere and everywhere. And it was just like teenage make out sessions – electric, exciting, desperate, and *limited*. I was the limiter. I hadn't told Anthony in words that I didn't want to move forward, but I told him with my body language, and he understood and respected my position. He also didn't communicate that in words. But his body respected the boundary. He didn't question it or make me talk about it. We'd made out at his cabin, in my cottage, in his SUV, in dark corners we could find when we were taking walks together, even in the little Co-op office once. I couldn't get past the make out stage because I knew once we moved on to sex, the clock started ticking on the expiration date of our relationship. I just didn't want that to happen.

I wanted to keep things exactly as they were and just ignore real life, but I also needed to talk to him about Ruthie. Did he know she was having health problems? Was I going to be violating her privacy and sharing really bad news with him?

"Maybe meet up for dinner instead?" I texted back.

"My place or yours?" His reply was quick and loaded with the usual suggestion that question carried.

"Nope. Somewhere we have witnesses," I texted. "I need to talk to you about something."

"I really dislike that kind of message," he texted back, "but name where and when. I'll be there."

We ended up at a woodfire pizza place that was making a name for itself as a microbrewery. I wasn't a beer drinker, but I knew it was casual and had nice corners for conversation. For some reason, I couldn't yet have dinner with Anthony at my favorite casual place – it felt too weird, having run into him there when I was on a date with Chris. Wrong somehow, which was just strange. And annoying since I loved that place.

"What's going on, Willow?" Anthony asked after he settled into his side of the cozy, high-backed booth. "You can't send me messages like that. I worried about you all afternoon. I almost came into the Co-op three times, but I knew that would just slow you down in getting out of there today."

"I'm sorry," I said. "I wasn't trying to worry you. But it is a worrisome topic. One you might know more about than I do." I looked at him hoping to see a spark of recognition. When I didn't, I spilled what Ruthie had shared with me quickly because the tension around Anthony's eyes was getting to me and, while I didn't expect the news to be any sort of relief for his worry, I didn't want the anxiety of anticipated bad news lingering.

"No," he finally said. "I didn't know anything about it. I knew she had an appointment last week, but I didn't think anything of it." In addition to the tension in his expression, he now also had that calculating look he often got when he was trying to problem-solve something.

"Surely Loren is on top of it. What did she say again? Something about stress and blood pressure?" he asked, trying to add everything up.

"Yes, that's all she really said, but stepping down suggests something serious." I reached across and gripped Anthony's hand. "She's going to be furious that I told you, but I thought you should know. And I really needed to talk to someone about it."

"Of course," he said, snapping out of wherever his brain had been and focusing on me. "Of course. What are you going to do? That Davis is a piece of work. When I was trying to gather some local business support for Spruce Lake, he wanted nothing to do with it. He's not my biggest fan. He actually tried to hire my firm when he was getting started with his hotel, but we didn't take the job. I didn't remember it, but he told me all about it. I hate to think of you having to add dealing with him to your already full plate."

"I don't know. I mean, what can I do? I've never had to do this without Ruthie, but I'll just have to move ahead. Figure out a way."

Anthony moved his beer to the side while the server put our pizza on the table. Anthony served each of us a slice and then took in a deliberate breath.

"Can we talk about another hard topic?" he asked, and immediately all my protective walls went up to the roof.

"Do we have to?" I tried to joke, blowing on my pizza.

"Willow, why can't we talk about your photography? It's an amazing thing. And I think it's good enough to be a full-time business. Why don't you want to talk about it?"

"There's nothing to talk about. It's just private, and I like it that way," I said, hoping he would let it go.

"Willow," he said in frustration. "Kitten," he tried again, flashing me a flirtatious smile. "I don't want to make you uncomfortable, but I want to understand. I did some digging online and saw that you do have some work at a few galleries. And I also know they put the right value on your art – unlike what you're charging for yourself at the Co-op. This is a viable business. You're so talented."

"Anthony, please," I begged. "Can we please not do this?"

"We're doing it. I know I made an ass out of myself – some of the comments I made about you not knowing what you had in the Co-op – as if you didn't understand how good the work was. And I know that was stupid and petty. In my defense, I was unknowingly doing pretty much anything I could to get a rise out of you back then. Anything to get you to engage with me."

His words were sweet, but I didn't buy it. "That is a lie, sir!" I said, hoping a good argument could derail this discussion. "You were not trying to engage with me when we met up at Ruthie's that first time. You were irritated that I wasn't the completely clueless cashier you thought I was. You were annoyed that you were wrong. I was still low on your importance meter; just not as low as you'd thought."

"What the - " Anthony's face scrunched into a scowl. "Willow, that's not true. That's not how I saw you then or now – or any time in between."

I liked the direction this discussion had taken. He'd completely forgotten about my photography.

"It is true. I know I don't rate in your professional world. I'm okay with that. But you were embarrassed."

"You've got it all wrong, Willow." His expression softened. "Yes, I was embarrassed. Because, yes, I'd been teasing you, and I'd gotten it wrong. But it's not like you're thinking. I didn't look down on you because of what I thought you did for a living. It's not that I thought it was better or worse than something else. It's just different – different from my experience. I was serious when I told you I wanted to kiss you that first time I met you. And that I found you fascinating. But I thought it was just on the level of 'this would be a fun fling.' I didn't imagine that we would have anything in common – or anything that could move beyond something physical. And when Ruthie introduced you, I had to question every assumption I'd made. And every way I'd stuck my foot in my mouth. So, yes, I was embarrassed, but I never looked down on you for what I *thought* you did for work. Will we ever be able to get past this thing – money, status, jobs… You know, none of that matters, right?"

I had a lot of things I wanted to say and felt my temper rising quickly. *Easy for you to say money and status doesn't matter. How can you sit there in your perfect, likely bespoke sweater that costs more than I make in a day and say none of those things matter? How can you even have a frame of reference? Privileged, clueless...* But I'd learned my lesson the last time I'd told him how I really felt about this topic. I knew his cluelessness wasn't cruel and that he was trying to put me at ease even if he was really achieving the opposite.

"Anthony, I don't think we should talk about this. I think we fundamentally disagree, and, while I like arguing with you about things that don't matter, I don't like this kind of arguing. I don't like arguing when neither of us will see it differently and when it will just end in hurt feelings. Can we just agree to disagree?"

"Willow," Anthony's eyes were tracking across my face. "This doesn't make sense. I just want to understand. I'm not trying to argue. You have a problem with this, that's clear. I'm trying to tell you that I don't, but you're telling me that I don't know myself. That you just get to think I'm some privileged jerk who can't see past these kinds of differences. That's not fair. I'm not telling you how to feel – at least I won't anymore. I'm just telling you how I feel."

I started scooting out of the booth. I needed to get out of there. I could feel my blood thumping in my chest. The few bites of pizza I'd taken felt like they were stuck in my throat. I felt trapped.

"Willow, stop," Anthony said as I put my jacket on and grabbed my bag. "Please," he said as I walked away.

He caught up to me before I could get all the way to my car. He came up to me from behind, took my hand, and matched my quick strides. "Willow, please," he said, "I just want to understand."

I stopped walking and pulled my hand back to myself. "You are never going to understand, and you have to stop asking."

We were on the edge of town, and the night was dark. There were fewer street lights on this end, and I was glad Anthony couldn't see my face clearly.

"Why? Why can't we talk about this?"

"The last time you pushed me on this stuff, you

stopped talking to me. You won't like what I have to say, so, please, can we just leave it?"

"I don't understand what the big deal is. This seems crazy. I'm not a moron, you know. Maybe I don't understand, but you could explain it and then I would."

"Fine. You want me to explain it?" I walked past my car and further into the darker side streets. I tried to expel my chaotic energy by taking quick, deliberate steps. "Look, you and Ruthie – you're so kind. You do your best. And you're right, you don't look down on other people. But you also don't understand because you can't. You can't understand what it's like to worry about a paycheck. Or about food or housing or a car that might or might not make it where you need to drive it. And most people who can't understand that do look down on it. They think you've done something to put yourself in that place. That you're lazy or stupid or less than."

Anthony stopped my frantic pace by gently gripping my elbow and slowing me down. "Willow, that's not true," he began.

"Oh my god!" I practically squealed. "See, this is why

we can't talk about this! You can't even imagine that this is real. That these things happen! Right after I graduated high school, my family lost our farm. Not lost it like couldn't find it. But that's what they call it – losing it." I stopped walking and looked out at a field along the side of the road. "What really happened is that someone took it. Bankers with money just take what isn't theirs. It doesn't matter how hard you work or how special something is or how much you give to it. The people with money get to decide, and they decided to take it. And everyone got to look on and pity us or make judgements about us. The rich bankers are the people who convinced my dad to keep mortgaging more than he could afford – to gamble with the only thing we had - in the name of expansion and progress and farming as a business. And then they got to decide he'd made poor choices. He's a good person, and he worked as hard as a person could work, but they got to take and they got to judge. And now you want to pick at it all those scabs and understand why I do what I do. I work, Anthony, because I have to. It's not a choice to be overworked and tired. I do photography because, yes, I love it, but also because I have to pay the mortgage for my parents' house. And I have to do it in secret because it's so shameful. I have to manipulate my parents' finances, so they won't know I'm helping them because there is shame in all of that." My voice caught on the word shame, and I had to stop and gather myself to shove the feelings back down. "It's something you will never understand. If you understood, you wouldn't keep asking – making me talk about it."

Anthony didn't say anything, and I knew we were back to the same place we'd been all those weeks ago when we had gone hiking and I'd gone off on him. There wasn't any coming back from this. It was just going to be awkward and uncomfortable. I could practically feel the dreaded pity coming out of his pores. I turned to go back to my car, and he walked with me, probably happy to be rid of me soon.

When we got there and I unlocked my door, he cupped my chin in his hand and turned my face to him. "I'm sorry I pushed," he said. Then he leaned in and kissed my lips softly. "Thank you for telling me." He let go and opened my door for me. "Be careful driving home," he said in a way that sounded a lot like "goodbye" to me as I shut the door and began to drive away.

Chapter 16

Sunshine let me know she had endured enough of my tossing and turning by jumping off the bed to go find a calmer place to sleep. I'd been trying to sleep for hours, but it just wasn't happening. I kept thinking about the consequences of my conversation with Anthony. He would be offended like he was the first time we talked about my feelings on the subject. And worse, now that he knew how ugly things were for me growing up, he would pity me. And it was just going to throw the balance off even more in our friendship. And it was even more clear to me now – the friendship wasn't going to make it.

I told myself it really didn't matter because I'd never really believed our friendship was going to make it anyway with this stupid friends with benefits idea.

And while I felt like Anthony completely lit me up on a physical, chemical level, the relationship - the friendship - was even more important to me. I wanted him in my life. And it just wasn't going to happen. And I'd stupidly accelerated the end. Why hadn't I just made up some dumb reason for keeping my photography a secret? He could have teased me about it incessantly and that would have been the end of it. But, no, I had to lose my cool and tell him the ancient history that didn't even matter anymore.

I turned to my other side again and counted the dwindling hours until I had to get up for work. I started punching my pillow when I heard a text alert on my phone. I willed my eyes to adjust to the light as I pulled up the message.

Anthony: I'm sorry. Really. I wish I could have that conversation over again.

Me: I wish we could make that conversation disappear.

Anthony: I can pretend it never happened if you want. Promise.

I smiled in relief as I considered his words. I knew

my outlook on this bothered him, but he wasn't going to give up on me this time. I also knew he meant it that he was willing to pretend if I needed him to. He didn't say things to me that he didn't mean. I took in the first full breath I'd taken since I had left him on the street.

Anthony: Willow? Are you asleep?

Me: No. Can't sleep.

Anthony: Would you be creeped out if I told you I was outside your house?

My eyes bugged out at his text. *What?* I quickly did a mental assessment of the state of my house and myself. The house was alright. Not great, but alright. Myself? I was sure I was a mess. I sat up on the side of the bed and reached for the pair of soft grey joggers I'd taken off before getting into bed. Then I quickly stood to grab a cardigan from my closet to go over my tank top. I drank half the glass of water that I now had a habit of taking to bed with me. Patting down my hair, I made my way to my front door and peeked out into the night.

Anthony stood in the moonlight looking sad but so, so handsome. He was in his running clothes and was rubbing the edge of his hand against the stubble on his face. I cracked the door open and when we locked eyes, Anthony mouthed the word, "Sorry." He gave me a second until I mouthed back, "Me, too."

I opened the door all the way, and Anthony pulled me into his strong hold. I wrapped my arms around his waist and squeezed tightly.

He murmured into my hair, "I'm sorry I pushed you too far."

I wasn't even listening to him. I was feeling his heartbeat and listening to his breath. I was just feeling him, and I wasn't in any hurry to stop.

He continued, "It's just, you know, if I could do something to fix things for you - I just want to fix it. I'm so sorry."

I froze.

"What?" he said, releasing me a bit. "Christ what did I say now? I'm going to get a muzzle for myself until I figure this out."

"Anthony, you can't *fix* me. This is my life. You can't fix my life. That says there's something broken about it. It's just my life, and it's different from yours and that's okay. How would you like it if I said something about your mother and how she is and said I wanted to fix it for you? That's just your life."

"Willow, I'm going to say something and then we're going to move on." He stroked down the length of my hair. "Kitten, you *are* trying to help me fix stuff with my mom, and I appreciate it. That's what this whole thing started as, right? That's all I'm trying to do... I'm not saying you're broken. God, you're not broken. You're perfect." He moved his hands under my hair and cradled the back of my head. "You're perfect, Willow - not broken at all."

I squeezed my eyes shut, willing any emotion back down. My chaotic mind kept swirling. I knew it didn't make sense to him. So many contradictions. But it made sense to me. And I just needed to keep everything to myself. It wasn't helping to try to make him understand. And I knew I could trust his intentions. I believed he was trying to help. I just... All these feelings – and talking about feelings. It was time to get back to my emotionless comfort zone.

"Do you work tomorrow?" he asked as he kept stroking my hair. "Of course, you work tomorrow. You should be asleep. God, I did this." He pulled back until we were only connected by our hands. "Can you sleep now? I should go. You need to sleep."

I knew it wasn't a smart move, but I did not want him to go home. I wanted to crawl right into my bed just the way we were and sleep all night and never get up.

"Anthony, I want you to stay," I said, looking down at our hands. "Could we - could you stay and could we just sleep?"

He gripped my chin and nudged it up until we were looking at each other. "Are you sure, Kitten?"

I gave a tiny nod and turned to my bedroom. It was stupid. I was stupid. I knew I was playing with fire, but I took my cardigan off and inched my joggers down until I was in my tank top and underwear next to my bed.

"Kitten, you said we were going to sleep. This isn't fair. I'll never sleep with that image burned in my brain." His eyes darted from my face to my chest. I knew my tank top was see through. I knew what he was seeing, but at that moment I wasn't thinking anymore. I wasn't thinking about the fight we'd had. I wasn't thinking about the future or the past. I wasn't thinking about our agreement or our relationship. I wasn't thinking about his mother or my mother or anything other than the man standing in front of me. He took a few steps toward me, and I gripped the bottom of his tee shirt, grazing his strong abs with my thumbs, and I started pushing it up and up.

"Willow, are you sure you want to do this?" His voice was deep and serious.

My eyes were fixed on every inch I was revealing of him, and I nodded my head silently.

"You're absolutely sure?" he asked one more time.

I looked up into his crystal eyes, nodded my head again, and was immediately overwhelmed by the swift shift in *everything*. Anthony grabbed his shirt behind his neck and pulled it off in a split second. He wrapped his arms around me and picked me up until I was hanging on to him, my legs wrapped around his waist.

And he started feasting.

I knew Anthony was intense, and I knew he burned hot. I knew he also had incredible control and restraint, and I'd been witnessing all those qualities each time we were together, but this - the intensity and the heat *without* the control and restraint… It was like being too close to fireworks. Everything was too loud, too close, too raw. And it was perfect.

"Condom," he said.

I kept kissing along his neck.

"Kitten, tell me you have a condom."

Anthony's urgent tone brought things back into focus. "Yes, I think so. Bathroom," I said, taking his bottom lip between mine.

He walked us into my small bathroom and placed me on the counter next to the sink. He kept kissing me, but asked, "Where? Where are they?"

I slapped my hand against the drawer next to me a few times. Anthony separated from me enough to open the drawer and start shifting the contents around. "I don't see anything," he said in frustration.

I pushed a few things out of the way until I saw the small, unopened package. "Here," I said, victorious.

He smiled and snapped them up. "I think I'm glad the box is unopened," he said. "And hard to find."

"And I think I'm glad you don't walk around with a condom in your wallet," I returned.

"That's changing after today," he growled as he picked me up again and walked back to the bed. He tossed me onto it and we both laughed. We kept laughing as he stripped down to his dark boxer briefs and joined me on the bed.

But then the kissing started again. And the burning. And the desperation. He helped me out of my tank top and kissed and sucked and stroked until I thought I would lose my mind.

I could feel how ready he was as we writhed against each other and helped each other out of the rest of our clothes. I pulled his face back up to mine and kissed him.

"Anthony, please," I said in between frenzied kisses.

"God, Willow, you're so precious," he said, worshipfully. He glided his fingers over every part of me until I couldn't take it anymore. I took him in my hand, and he groaned into my neck. "Christ, Willlow. God, that feels so good. You feel so good." He pulled back just enough to deal with the condom, and then anticipation met reality. We connected and it felt like it had never felt before – meant something it had never meant before. He wasn't kissing me anymore. He'd gone still and was watching me, a question in his expression.

I nodded at him that it was good. That I was fine. That I was ready.

As he started to move, my mind went blank. I just felt. Felt how much I cared for him. Felt how right this was.

He responded to my every desire, to my every cue. Just like the burning fireworks, we were approaching our peak. Anthony growled a strangled cry as we came together, and I relished the feel of his weight as he burrowed into my neck, kissing and saying sweet things like, "Amazing" and "This is my favorite place" and "Finally."

As the haze started to clear, my thoughts started to become more focused again. And those thoughts made my chest feel tight. Afraid to give Anthony a window into my feelings, I slid from under him a bit onto my side. He wrapped himself around me and cradled my back into his solid chest.

I knew casual relationships had an expiration date because someone always wanted more. I let the tears silently fall as I gripped Anthony's arm. I just never imagined the someone who wanted more would be me.

Chapter 17

This was a disaster. I thought back to my past relationships and how bad I'd felt each time I'd had to end things. I knew the other person had developed feelings, and I had felt bad about that – about hurting their feelings. But, until now, I hadn't understood that I hadn't felt bad enough. I hadn't understood that worrying about their hurt feelings was the least of the considerations. I'd really been destroying their hopes, crushing how they wanted to go through life. Because I now knew: this was agony.

Of course, I had known that I liked Anthony – valued his friendship, enjoyed spending time with him. And, of course, I knew I was attracted to him. But those things did not add up to love or a future or all the crazy places my mind was going now. But putting down my walls – being truly vulnerable for just a moment in time had changed everything. Revealed everything. I was completely and utterly in love with Anthony Kaplan.

How could this happen to me? To me?! The queen of casual. The champion of compartmentalizing feelings. My mother was right. Not that there would be a magic moment with a happily ever after. But that I would know when I knew. And, God, did I know.

I didn't know how I was going to survive being around him, but I also didn't know how I would survive not being around him. The morning after THE NIGHT THAT CHANGED EVERYTHING, we'd both woken to Sunshine walking across our entwined bodies, asking for her breakfast. We'd laughed and focused our attention on her and avoided talking about what had happened. I'd found Anthony a new toothbrush, we'd eaten some breakfast, and I'd headed to work.

He had texted later in the day, and I'd agreed to having dinner at his place, which had escalated into another night together – this one with even less sleep than the night before as we had learned each other's bodies and preferences. And with my alarm set for very early so I could go home and check in with Sunshine before work. Anthony had grumbled that next time we were bringing her with us.

I knew Anthony was enjoying himself. I knew he cared about me, and apparently found me attractive. But what he was doing to me went beyond what I saw happening with him. He was changing my life – with every caress, every stroke, every kiss – I felt it all to the corners of my soul. While he was... enjoying himself.

I had determined that I needed him to go back to Boston or New York. I needed him in smaller doses if I was going to maintain any sort of friendship with him without ruining it by revealing my desire for more. I knew better than anyone how uncomfortable it was to be on the other side of that. We had the upcoming Spruce Lake event to finish helping Emerson with, and I was going to start encouraging Anthony to get back to his real life once that was done. Let him know he'd made a difference he could feel good about, and it would last even if he wasn't around all the time to keep things going.

Our next event was an Open Farm Locavore Day that

would happen the first week in November – less than a few weeks away. I had given Anthony the list of farmers who might consider leading a workshop or a Q & A session. He was checking in with them to organize an agenda. The trick was trying to organize something that made money but also had some benefit for the farmers agreeing to participate. I was working with food vendors who would set up in the dining hall for the event. Emerson and Ruthie were working on marketing. The goal was to get people who were interested in local food or farming to come pay an all-day admission fee that gave them access to workshops, demonstrations, and the grounds of the camp.

"I got Max Parker!" Anthony's voice shook me out of my distracted thoughts. I was straightening up in the Co-op café and when I turned, Anthony was standing in front of me with a big smile on his face. I had to rewind what he'd said in my mind and try to focus on that rather than how a smiling Anthony made me feel.

"For the workshop?" I asked, turning to continue with my work.

"Yes. He's a really interesting guy actually. It

started making me think about some things I've been wondering about for my foundation."

I made some murmuring sounds to make it seem like I was invested in the conversation, but really I was just thinking how much it hurt to look at him and know he could never feel for me what I felt for him.

"Willow, are you listening to me?"

I turned to Anthony and forced myself to focus. And to rewind the conversation again. "Yeah, of course, I am. Your foundation, right?"

"Yeah, I never thought about some of the access and start-up issues Max mentioned. I want to talk it over with my CFO. I think there might be something there."

This agony needed to stop, and Anthony was giving me a good opening. "That's really great," I said, trying to inject energy into my words. "You'll probably need to head back to Boston soon then to move things along, right? If you need to go, I know we can manage the event. Just give me the basics, and I can work through the final details with Max."

Anthony didn't say anything, which forced me to really focus on his face. The merry twinkle he usually had in his eyes had dimmed, and his smile had fallen. "Are you trying to get rid of me, Willow?"

"No," I lied. "Of course not. I'm just saying we can't expect you to keep your life on a permanent pause just for the music camp. I'm sure Ruthie never meant for that to happen. And besides, you've brought in funding and resources already for the facilities improvements. You don't have to be on site for that. I'm just saying, I'm sure you have important things to do. Things that aren't here," I finished in a mumble.

Anthony cocked his head to the right as he looked at me questioningly. "Right," he finally said. "I think I'm fine staying here for now – at least until the next event is finished." He shook his head like he was shaking the thoughts away. "I almost forgot. I stopped by because I brought you something."

He started digging in his bag until he pulled out a small box with a familiar logo on it along with a sparkly pink bundle of straps.

"Chocolate and... What is this?" I asked, taking the beautiful box of specialty chocolate Anthony was handing me.

"This," he said, forming a shape with his hands in the middle of the straps, "is for Sunshine. I know she doesn't need a new one, but I saw it and thought it would be fun. Maybe we can go for another hike soon."

My heart was not going to survive this man.

I took the halter from him and mumbled a thanks as I considered how perfect this moment would be if only he could love me back a little. And how painful it was to know that he never could.

He took my chin beneath his thumb and finger and lifted my face until my eyes met his. "Are you okay, Kitten? Is there something going on?"

"I'm fine," I tried a smile, but I could feel the tension in it. "Really."

"You can tell me if something's - "

"Willow," Brendan approached, and I felt relief at the interruption even after hearing what it was about. "Bill Davis is here and wants to talk to you."

∞∞∞

"Well, this is a pleasure!" Ruthie said as she opened

her door wide for me to come in. "If visits like this are what come from stepping down, I should have done it a long time ago."

I hugged Ruthie quickly, thinking how strange the change in our relationship was. I had always valued her as my mentor – had always cared about her. But now, knowing about her health and having spent time with her and her family... with Anthony... It was like I hadn't allowed my feelings about our relationship to go beyond some professional shield. Now I hugged her and hoped that she could feel how much I cared about her. How much I loved her and worried for her.

"Let's settle in over here," Ruthie indicated to a little sitting area that looked out over the lake. She had a beautiful tea service set out. The tea pot was steaming and there were mouthwatering pastries piled on top of each other. My mom's chipped plates flashed through my mind, and I told myself just because it was different didn't make either thing wrong. Didn't make one uppity and one shameful. They were just different experiences. I was really trying to tamp down my knee-jerk reactions after the conversation I'd had with Anthony.

"This is lovely, Ruthie. Thank you."

"So, to what do I owe the honor?"

"Well," I began. "It's just some work stuff. But it's not important. How are you feeling?" I took in her appearance. She looked every bit the adorable elderly firecracker she usually did, but there was more of a sag in her posture, more tiredness in her eyes. I couldn't stress her out by sharing my reaction to my conversation with Bill Davis. That had been the reason I'd asked to meet with her, but I'd quickly realized how unfair that was. I could make up something simple to talk about like supplier logistics or some of Brendan's latest antics. I couldn't stress her out with the real stuff.

"Willow, if I could have kept Loren's concerns from you, I would have. But just because it's good for me to let go of that responsibility of battling with Bill Davis, it doesn't mean you can stop talking to me about it. If you cut me out of what's going on, I'll die of boredom. And concern for you, which is it's own kind of stress. I can manage being a support for you. And I need to be kept in the loop. What the heck is going on?" She gave me that stern look that always got her everything she wanted.

"Oof. Fine," I gave in, torn about whether I should actually hold back or give her what she was asking for. "He wanted to meet with me today. It didn't go well. He said he knew about all the extra work I'd been doing to help out at Spruce Lake, and he said I needed to stop using my –" I braced myself before repeating what he had said. It had angered me so much, and I knew how it would hit Ruthie. "He said I needed to stop using my energy and resources for anything except the Co-op."

"He what?" Ruthie's voice was piercing in the serene room. And she didn't stop ranting for a full minute, talking about his nerve and how he couldn't control what I did and how she had a mind to go to the next meeting even though she'd gone ahead and officially stepped down even before the election.

I sat in horror, watching her reaction. I had known it was going to be bad, but I guess our new, closer relationship also removed even the small filter she must have brought to the Co-op before. Unfiltered Ruthie was fierce. And I couldn't stop worrying about her blood pressure.

"Ruthie," I said as she finally stopped to take a

breath. "Please, Ruthie. Don't get so worked up. Please?" I nudged her cup of tea toward her. "I am one hundred percent fine. You taught me to be fine. I can handle him. I promise. I just need a little advice. That's all. I don't need you to worry about me or fight the battles for me." I surprised myself with my next statement. "You gave me the tools to do that." It was true, although I hadn't really believed it until now.

We looked at each other and began to smile.

"Of course, you can, Willow," she said. She took a sip of her tea and gave me a look that seemed filled with pride. "I have always known that. I just needed you to know it, too."

"Thank you," I said, wiling my shining eyes to not spill over with tears. This vulnerability door I had opened was overwhelming.

"So, what do you need advice about? How can I help?"

"I think I already know the answer – I guess I would just feel better bouncing it off you."

"Bounce away."

"So, no one can tell me what to do in my off time. Even if the connections I have are related to my work.

As long as I don't cross any lines asking for people to do something for Spruce Lake in exchange for something at the Co-op. Or anything like that, right? As long as the two stay totally separate, it's no one's business what I do outside of work, right? And just because Bill wants me to go back to working twenty-four/seven doesn't mean that I should. I've really been reading up on management material, and I know I'm not actually setting a good example for other people by not modeling a good work/life balance. I guess I just need to hear that I'm not out in left field."

"No, Willow," Ruthie said, topping off my cup of tea. "You're right where you need to be. You're level-headed and your ethical radar is spot on. He can't push you around. And what will he do if you resist? Fire you? I'd like to see him try."

We laughed at the idea of the Co-op without me working there. I had become a constant there, and everyone knew it. But the laughter turned a little sad for both of us because there was something tragic in that thought. That my life was so tied to that place that it was unimaginable I wouldn't be there. Even for all of

Ruthie's commitment to the place, she was able to step down and the day-to-day didn't change.

Ruthie took in a deep breath and said, "But just because he can't push you out doesn't mean you shouldn't consider what you want. You don't have to stay, Willow. I'm not trying to talk you into leaving. I love that place, and it gives me comfort that you're still in charge, but I also care about you. And, while we were making some strides in getting a better work/life balance for you, I don't want you to hate work. I don't want you to have to battle with the board all the time. You are so talented and could find different work if you wanted to."

I opened my mouth to respond, but Ruthie broke in again. "Just consider it."

"Now," she said, "tell me about how things are going with my nephew."

"I actually did want to talk to you about Anthony," I said, "but I'm not sure you're going to like what I have to say."

Ruthie's face fell, and it hurt my heart. She was totally going to blame me for this.

"I just don't want you to get your hopes up. Anthony and I… We have an understanding. We are really good friends. I promise you that is the most important things for both of us – that we are friends. Our relationship beyond that is casual. I really like him. And I think he likes me, but we also understand each other. We know there's no future in it, so we are trying to make sure we keep our friendship intact when we get to the point that anything beyond that ends."

Ruthie just looked at me and didn't say anything at all.

"It's mutual, Ruthie. I need you to know that. I promise it isn't me trying to hurt him. Also, for what it's worth – I'm not the… the maneater you seem to think I am." I was getting a little miffed the more I explained myself. Why did she have this opinion of me? And how was I going to convince her that I didn't have the ability to break Anthony's heart?

"You silly thing," Ruthie finally said. "I know you're not a maneater. I tease you because you keep dating these silly boys. These men who have the maturity of a turnip. Anthony is not one of your boys."

"I've noticed."

"And it delights me to see your friendship. He's precious to me." Ruthie pointed her finger at me and said, "But so are you, my dear. I adore you. I care about you as if you were my own daughter. I trust both of you and no matter what happens, I will love both of you."

The damn vulnerability was breaking me wide open, and I couldn't stop the tears from streaming.

"You sweet girl, did you really think I would blame you if things didn't work out? Like I said, Anthony isn't one of your boys. He would never blame you or want me to take sides."

"I think I knew that somewhere deep down but thank you for saying it." I wiped my eyes with the napkin from the table.

"But I do worry about you. About both of you. Anthony is… Well, the way he grew up. Has he told you about it?"

I nodded but urged her to go on. I was eager to hear anything about Anthony that she wanted to share.

"I did my best to make up for what was lacking in his own home. My brother – and even more his wife –

they just didn't take an interest. It was heartbreaking to watch. Anthony was a little man by the age of twelve. He took care of himself all on his own. Even when I would have him visit in the summer, I would have to convince him to relax. He would have lived on cereal and peanut butter and jelly because he could make it himself and clean up after himself. He has always taken care of himself, and it's made it hard for him to allow anyone else to do it. It makes him uncomfortable."

I nodded because I could see that. He was always making me coffee. He was always trying to feed me or see if there was anything I needed. And when I tried to flip things, he quickly flipped it right back. Taking care of people was my comfort zone because it's what I'd always had to do, but Anthony hadn't allowed me to do that. I hated that I hadn't pushed it harder.

"He is so agreeable and affable that people often don't notice he's keeping them at arm's length."

I nodded again – everything Ruthie was saying checked out. "He does do that." I thought about the times he'd pushed me to share things about myself. I had done it coupled with emotional outbursts. When

Anthony shared, he was clinical – like he didn't allow himself to dwell on what he was sharing or really share the emotional pieces of his experience. And he took such easy charge of everything that he didn't give you a chance to even notice how he was steering all the time. He was "letting" me help him with his mom. But I knew better. He could handle her, and he didn't need my help to do it. Who knows why he roped me into this thing, but he was very clearly in charge. And now that I was broken open into a vulnerable mess of feelings, I wanted him there with me.

∞∞∞

Two could play this game. Anthony had brought me chocolate and a harness for Sunshine. I could get him a gift and he would have to graciously accept. I'd been thinking a lot about what Ruthie had said. I'd spent my life taking care of other people, and it had been nice to have Anthony not needing that from me. I hadn't even really realized that was part of what made me feel so good around him. I was the girl who took care of others, and he was the guy who always took care of himself. But now I wanted to take care of him – not because it was my role and he needed it but because I loved him and wanted him to know he was cared for. It completely broke my heart to think about his lessons as a child that taught him he only had himself to rely on.

"It's for your music," I said as I handed him the leather bound journal. "I mean I'm not exactly sure how you'll use it, but I thought if you wrote down chords or things for songs. Or if you ever wrote things of your own. I don't know. I just wanted you to know how much I appreciate you and how talented I think you are. I know you're really modest about your playing –"

Anthony raised an eyebrow and I continued. "And with your ego," I adopted a teasing expression and tone, "that's saying something. I'm not sure why it's this area that you're modest about, but I just wanted to tell you you're great." I lamely finished. "You're really great."

Anthony took the book from me and flicked through the thick, cream pages. Then he lifted his hand and gently pushed my hair back from my shoulder and softly began stroking the side of my neck as he looked at me with an expression I hadn't yet seen. He looked young and sweet. I was getting the tiniest glimpse of his feelings, and they were tender and breathtaking. "Thanks, Kitten," he said as he leaned in to kiss me. "I'll write something for you in here." He wrapped me up in his arms, and I felt his grip on the book at my lower back.

"You don't have to," I said into his precious chest.

"But I will." He kissed the top of my head before letting me go. "Later though. We should probably take off."

We were headed to Spruce Lake for the Open Farm Locavore Day. The hard work had been done, and hopefully today we would be able to enjoy things. There had been a respectable number of pre-event ticket sales, and we were hoping for a bigger turnout due to some last-minute advertising.

After we arrived, Anthony took off to go make sure things were set up in the classroom where the workshops would be held, and I went to check in with the food vendors. We had a few who had their own trucks, like Luisa, but most of them were set up at tables around the perimeter of the dining hall. There was everything from local beef jerky to an array of hand-iced, farm-themed sugar cookies. The vendors had gone all out, and I really hoped it was a good day for them.

Anthony and I met up again at Lanie Parker's table. He and Max Parker approached together, having settled everything for Max's upcoming presentation. I knew how much Lanie loved to bake sweet things, but she was totally representing Max's organic vegetable farm today with her boxed lunches. She had hearty root veg salads with cornbread from cornmeal I knew had been milled from Max's crop. Max formally introduced Lanie to Anthony, and Anthony commented on how much he loved the prepared meals Lanie sold at the Co-op.

"Thank you," Lanie said in her soft voice. "I love cooking with the food we grow."

Max put his arm around his shy wife and gave her a comforting squeeze.

"This is some of that diversification you were talking about, right Max?" Anthony asked as he sampled one of the little squares of cornbread Lanie had put on a plate at the edge of her table.

"Yes, although this area is all Lanie. That wasn't any part of my vision. It's all her."

"Max was telling me about the farm shares and the project he has with the ag program at the local college," Anthony said, looking at me. "I think some of these types of innovative ideas for farmers would be a great area for my foundation. Some forgivable loans could give small farmers the ability to move forward with their vision. Max has agreed to try to help me figure out what could really help."

"I think it could be groundbreaking," Max chimed in. "I definitely had some factors that allowed me to move forward with my projects. I'd love to see what could come of more seed money for other farmers around here. Of course, it didn't hurt that I ended up on such a great piece of land. Your dad built something really great, Willow." Max kindly put the words out there, but Anthony froze next to me. I could feel his tension, so I quickly said, "Thanks, Max. It's amazing where you've taken it. Anthony, I think we need to go see if Ruthie has arrived."

I pulled him away from Lanie's table quickly, looking

back to see confused expressions on Lanie and Max's faces.

"That guy?" Anthony finally said after I'd guided him away from the event area. "That's the guy who took your farm?"

Anthony's jaw was like granite. I could feel how his entire body was rigid, and I tried to relax him by rubbing from his shoulders and around his neck.

"No, Anthony. Max didn't take the farm. Calm down."

"I'll get it back for you," he said. "That's an easy fix. I just can't believe I let that guy almost worm his way into my foundation as a consultant."

I started to giggle a little, and Anthony looked at me like I was crazy. "This is funny now? I'll make him pay, Willow. I promise you."

I really started to laugh at that point. "Anthony, Max Parker did not take my farm. Max bought the farm from the bank. And he tried really hard to make it look to everyone like he was just buying it – he tried to keep the foreclosure a secret. Good grief, he even tried to get the bank to agree to deed the property back to my dad so he could buy it from him fair and square. I honestly think he wanted to pay more for it if the money would have gone straight to my dad instead of the bank. You can't be mad at Max Parker. He's one of the nicest people in the world."

Anthony looked annoyed at my words about Max and sullenly said, "I could still get it back for you."

I felt his words and his intent like the gut-wrenching kindness it was. I cradled his dear face in my hands and stood on my tip toes to kiss him. "You are the best man I know," I said, kissing him again. He cupped my elbows, and I said, "Thank you because I know you mean it. But I don't want the farm back. It wouldn't fix the hurt. And it's Max and Lanie's home now. It hasn't been my home in a long time."

As Anthony looked down at me with his invested and caring gaze, the chip on my shoulder gave way to honest feelings. "In the end, it was probably good. My dad worked too hard. My mom never loved farm life. I've learned more about myself by working at the Co-op and working on my photography business than I was likely to learn without those experiences. And, honestly, I know it's not the bank's fault. Not anyone's fault really.

I know that I have to really work through that trauma. That's really the issue. I'm sorry it's spilled onto you so many times. And thank you for helping me."

Anthony gathered me into his arms, and I wondered again how I would ever survive letting go of this closeness we had. How I would ever survive just being his friend. I felt all the genuine concern he had for me as he embraced me, and I wished for the millionth time that you could make a person love you.

Chapter 18

This was the day I had been dreading. The day I had finally resolved to be the day I needed to encourage Anthony to go back to his real life. To start the conversation that it was time to transition back to being friends. I just couldn't keep myself on high alert anymore for the heartbreak that was looming. I needed to rip off the band-aid and get through the transition, hoping Anthony and I could be the exception to the rule. That if I could hide my true feelings, Anthony would still be comfortable being my friend.

My parents had invited us to their house for dinner. I couldn't even be nervous about how my mother would behave because I was so distracted by how to approach things with Anthony. And I trusted him with my mom in a way that I didn't trust anyone else. I knew he wouldn't hold her behavior against her – or against me. Plus, she had stars in her eyes when she looked at Anthony. She thought this was my happily ever after.

"It seems Spruce Lake is going to be just fine," Anthony said. We were finishing dinner and we'd been telling my parents about the success of the events, the building projects, and future events that Emerson now had on the books for the off-season. "My Aunt Ruth is a special woman," Anthony said. I squeezed his thigh under the table, knowing he was worried about her health. "And she knew bringing in Willow would make a difference."

"And you," I said quickly.

"Well, we make a good team," Anthony said, smiling sweetly at me.

I spared a nervous glance at my mother. She wasn't at her best. I'd tried to steer the topic of conversation to her a few times because it was clear to me she thought she was being excluded. In reality, we'd been having good general conversation over dinner. We had talked about some things at my dad's store, Anthony had asked about my mom's family and how my parents had met, we'd laughed at some of Sunshine's latest antics. But I knew my mother. And I knew she was bored with our conversation and didn't feel like we were paying enough attention specifically to her. I was eager to get through dessert and leave, although I felt bad for the night my dad had ahead of him. I knew it wasn't likely to be a good one.

I watched in horror as she screwed up her face and suddenly smacked her hand on the table in the middle of the continued conversation between Anthony and my dad about how well things were going at Spruce Lake. "It must be so easy to fix problems when you're rich as God. People like you don't even know what real problems are."

Silence.

But silence never stopped my mother. She enjoyed filling it when she was feeling neglected. She'd taken center stage and wouldn't let it go anytime soon.

I was mortified. And I hated that her choice of harsh words sounded like familiar ones to me. Jeez, was that how I had sounded when I'd blown up at Anthony?

"Anthony, I'm sorry. Why don't we head out?"

"It's fine, Willow," he said, patting my hand. "I'm fine." He turned to my mom and said, "I understand what you mean, and you're right. My role in this project has been very easy. I've not denied that. Willow and some others have done the heavy lifting. I'm lucky to be a part of it."

To a normal person, this would have been the end of an awkward outburst. But that wasn't how my mom operated. Seeing Anthony wasn't an easy target by a direct hit, she set her sights on me.

"Pfft. Heavy lifting? Willow? She just likes the attention. She's a typical daddy's girl. She learned how to work hard just to take his attention away from me."

This tactic hit its mark and everyone was trying to respond at once. I was pleading with her to be quiet, my dad was begging her to go to the kitchen with him to start the coffee, but Anthony's booming voice overpowered us. "Wait!," he said as my dad was trying to usher her out of her chair. "With all due respect, Mrs. Miller, I can't listen to you berate your daughter. She's an amazing woman, and I won't hear you demean her and lash out at her just because you have some problems."

"I have some problems? Ha! You're going to have some problems, mister, if you take her on. But be my guest. Save the princess. Hand it all to her on a silver platter just like her father does."

"Are you kidding me? Willow, let's go." Anthony stood from the table, but my mother wasn't even close to finished.

"That's right. Little Martyr Willow – always makes herself look so giving, but she really is just out to get what she can. Get all the attention. All the breaks."

"That's enough!" Anthony shouted.

"Anthony, please, let's just go," I said pulling at his sleeve.

"No, Willow. I know there are some issues here, but this isn't okay. The two of you," Anthony said in a voice that had us all frozen in our places. "The two of you have no idea what your daughter does for you, and yet you let this problem spill over onto her."

"Anthony, please," I said, willing him to keep his mouth shut.

"Your daughter works two jobs to be able to support herself and you."

"Stop," I said quietly, putting pressure on Anthony's arm.

But he was just getting started. "She pays your mortgage and I'm sure a lot more. And she jumps through every hoop so that you will never know."

"Anthony, stop," I said more loudly this time.

"She props you both up. Do you know how fucked up that is? That your daughter supports you both financially and emotionally?"

"Stop!" I shouted, pressing my hands over my ears. I thought I was going to lose my mind watching my father crumble in front of me.

"Critter?" my dad whispered.

"Anthony, you need to leave." I started to push him toward the door.

"Willow, you shouldn't have to –"

"Now!" I raised my voice again. "You don't understand anything here. My mom's right. You don't know what real problems are, and you are making everything worse. Just go back to your real life. You don't understand this one, and I want you to leave us alone."

I looked around and saw the pain on everyone's faces, felt the tears on my own. "Just leave, Anthony."

Chapter 19

How do you come back from the worst humiliation? The ultimate shame, the biggest disappointment, the shattering of trust? I had come to the conclusion that you didn't. You just kept going – pretending that the disappointment was expected. Pretending that you hadn't been hoping for something great – secretly, in that tiny place beneath all your fears.

My dad was broken. He had so many great qualities, but his way of coping with hard things had always been to go along with the hard stuff - never to brace against it, to fight against it. He just went along with it like the current carrying him – even if it was a direction he really didn't want to go if he had stopped to think about it. He was going with this new reality, but he did not like it. Anthony's words had broken him. We'd had a few conversations since the big blowup, but we'd gotten to the point where we now just ignored the fact that he'd lost much of his clueless positivity – that if my mom were to break down, he might just break down with her.

My mom was angry. She was embarrassed. But she was holding it together. It was like she finally understood that her choices and behavior had consequences outside of herself. She'd made an appointment to discuss her medication. She wasn't happy about it, and she held Anthony accountable for everything bad in the world, but she had at least agreed to do it. She was still frosty with me, and it was clear she was only doing it for my dad. I didn't care much that she wouldn't do it for me. I was just glad she was doing it.

My coping mechanism was familiar. I worked. I forced myself to drink plenty of water, but I had no appetite. I lay in my bed, but I didn't sleep much. And when I did, I heard staticky noises and saw black swaths of space punctuated by piercing flashing lights. Like a thunderstorm that never quite arrived but also never left.

And Anthony? Well, he'd done a vanishing act. He

had clearly heard me when I told him to leave. He must have walked out of my parents' house and headed straight back to Boston.

It had been a week. I wasn't having problems at work because I just didn't care. If Brendan was slacking or when Bill Davis had something to say, it was just part of the backdrop of my day. I stocked, I talked to vendors, I ran numbers, I sent emails. I did it all. The part that was different was I avoided Ruthie. I knew she said she wouldn't be mad, but I had shouted at Anthony. Told him again that he didn't get what it was like to live in the real world. Backtracked on all the progress we'd made. The progress I was starting to make. This wasn't us deciding it was time to shift back into friends. This was me telling him off in the worst possible way.

I couldn't believe he'd told my parents about the mortgage. I couldn't believe he'd yelled at them like he had. But when I rewound it in my mind, how could I hold onto all of my anger? I still had plenty of it. He had no right to reveal that – to hurt my parents like that. But I knew what he was trying to say – that they shouldn't hurt me in certain ways either. I knew he was trying to stick up for me. And what did I do? Tell him to leave. I meant for him to leave right then. I didn't mean for him to leave forever. I wasn't making decisions in that moment. I was reacting. It had all been too much. I had needed it to stop, and it was my job to protect my parents.

It was my job to protect my parents.

I had checked my phone over and over the next day, but Anthony hadn't texted or called. I should have sent a message to him, but I was angry and dealing with the aftermath. My dad had told me to stop paying their bills immediately, and I'd told him that wasn't possible. He couldn't support them on his nearly minimum wage paycheck, and there was no way Mom could venture into the working world at this point in her life. He argued but there really weren't any other solutions. I reassured them both that I wasn't overworking because of them.

I had to tell them about my photography business and was able to be convincing in my assertion that I did it for fun and it was just lucky that it paid the extra bills. I was able to tell them truthfully that I would be doing it even if I didn't earn money from it. That was enough to satisfy my mom. My dad still struggled with it. The unfairness of a hard-working man who had to be ashamed his whole life because of money was sobering. This latest blow made it hard for him to keep his head up and be the cheerful support for my mom he normally was.

I missed my friend so much. I thought about reaching out to him every minute of every day, trying to imagine whether it would be welcome or not. I was considering it as I usually did when I pulled the mail out of my box at the end of a long day at work.

Right on top was a letter from the bank, which was unusual since it was too early for the next month's mortgage statement. Just the reminder of the stupid mortgage and all the things it represented had me throwing the letter on my kitchen table and distracting myself with other things. I fed Sunshine, I worked on some photos, and I tried to gather the energy to make myself some dinner. I ultimately picked at some cheese and crackers and called it good. I kept eyeing the letter from the bank and it kept making me crankier. I knew it was just the annual escrow statement or something like that, but it was this symbol that was just making my mood worse.

Finally, I sat down at the kitchen table and opened the letter. I pulled the folded piece of paper out only to see my check fall from it. Sunshine hopped onto the table and walked across the check. *What was going on? Had my check bounced somehow?* I opened the letter and lost my breath as I read that the bank thanked me for my business and for faithfully paying the mortgage that had now been paid in full.

That son of a bitch.

∞ ∞ ∞

The next morning, I headed straight for the bank. They were going to wire that money straight back to Anthony Kaplan's account. He couldn't do this!

"Willow, I'm not sure what you're talking about," Tammy Larkins, the head teller said.

"You have to send the money back to Mr. Kaplan," I said again. "He can't pay off the mortgage just because he wants to. It's in my name. And my dad's. You can't just take a payment from anyone."

"I'm sorry, Willow, but we actually can. I can't stop someone from making a payment. I can't give out any information about the account, but if someone makes a payment against a loan, I wouldn't actually stop that from happening. And I can't just send it to someone now. The loan is paid off."

"Fine. I want to take out a new loan, and I want the proceeds sent to the bank account that the final payment came from."

"Well, that would take some time, but... Look, I don't know what's going on, but I've pulled up the payment history and the final payment came from your dad."

∞∞∞

"Calm down, Critter," my dad said to me. He'd asked my mom to give us some privacy when I pounded on their door, which she hadn't liked at all. Now we sat in their small kitchen, and it was clear my dad knew this was coming.

"What did you do, Dad? How did you pay the mortgage? Please tell me you didn't take out a shady loan or something. Please tell me we can fix this."

"I didn't take out a shady loan. I promise there's nothing to fix."

My dad lifted his eyes to mine. He shifted in his seat and finally said, "I made a deal with Anthony Kaplan."

I hadn't thought I could feel more uncomfortable than I had in all the times Anthony and I had hit upon this particular issue, but I found I could. I felt my chest tighten and my skin burn like there were a thousand needles poking every part of my body. I had no control over anything in my life anymore. That man had decided everything. He'd gotten his way as a parting gift to himself, celebrating the end of our friendship. He could set me up in a way that eased his mind and then go about his merry way.

But I didn't want to be set up the way he wanted me to be set up. I wanted my comfort zone back. I took care of people, dammit. Especially these people.

"Critter, just listen," my dad coaxed. He didn't look great - but better than he had been looking this past week. "Anthony and I want the same thing. We want the best for you. You know I don't want to take a handout like that from anyone, but I did it for you. I argued with him. I tried to think of anything I could do for him to earn that money. But what could I really do? What could he need from me?"

"Dad, we can give it back. I can get another loan and we can give it back to him. We are doing just fine. Aren't we? I can totally manage. I have a job and a side hustle. That's not unusual. We are fine!"

"We are fine thanks to you, Willow. But if I can take this one thing off your plate by eating some humble pie, I'm going to do it. You've been propping us up for too many years. We all got used to it, and it needs to change. Anthony's right about that."

"How are you having these conversations with him, Dad? Please tell me you're not still talking to him. After what he did? After what he said?"

"He said things that needed to be said. I should have never let it get to the point that someone had to say those things to me. That was my fault, not his."

"I don't want this. You are not helping me by doing

this."

"Look, he said something about his foundation and helping farmers. I did try to talk him out of it, but he said that his foundation is set up to help farmers out and that includes farmers who ran into problems and hard times. He said the money was earmarked for a farmer."

He was such a smooth operator. It shouldn't have surprised me he was going to get his way.

"Critter, he gave me something for you."

"You saw him?"

"Yes, he came to the house a few days ago, and we talked through things. We went to the bank together and he put the money in my account, so I could write the check myself."

My mind raced, wondering if he was still in town.

"Here, he wanted me to give this to you once things were settled." He handed me a folded, familiar cream-colored piece of paper. Paper from the journal I had given to Anthony.

"He said to read it when you were ready."

Chapter 20

I was never going to be ready for Anthony's letter. I knew what it was going to say. Goodbye. In some form or other, he was saying goodbye to me. It was exactly what I'd been trying to avoid by keeping my feelings from him. In the end, my love for him hadn't mattered at all. Our differences, rather than any revelation I had fallen for him, had been enough to blow up the friendship.

Once my anger finally exhausted itself, I just felt regret. Regret that I hadn't been able to handle the situation better. Remorse that I hadn't been able to accept my situation without all the shame and secrecy around it, which is what had opened everything up to this unnecessary outcome.

Why had I thought handling my parents was doing

anything other than enabling all of their tendencies and shielding them from responsibility? Yes, I wanted to spare them pain, but I also had done everything I could to prevent them from having to face their own shortcomings and how those impacted me.

If I had come to that realization sooner, maybe Anthony could have had more patience with me. No, that wasn't right. He was always patient. Maybe I just wouldn't have pushed him away. He held up a mirror to my situation, and I hadn't liked it, so I did what I could to break the mirror. But I missed him so much. He hadn't just been a cruel mirror; he had been the best kind of friend. Someone who held up the mirror, but only did it because he wanted me to be happier. Someone who supported and encouraged me. Someone who felt my situation so keenly himself that he couldn't tolerate it for me.

"I knew it was you all along," Ruthie said.

A few weeks had passed. Ruthie had tracked me down at work because I'd been brushing off her emails and voice messages inviting me to meet up. I wasn't proud of it. I was worried about her, and I missed her.

But I just couldn't talk to her about Anthony yet.

Ruthie being Ruthie – she wasn't used to taking no for an answer, so today she'd tracked me down when she knew I would be working and insisted I go have lunch with her. Insisted – including her using the words *I insist*.

I had just given her the short version of things that had happened, including the bit about my photography.

"You did not know," I said, astounded.

"Willow, you're not a very good liar. Every time we had to discuss the anonymous artist who preferred to be paid in cash, your voice would get quieter, and you wouldn't meet my eyes. You would shuffle papers and repeat everything twice. Plus, I know Mr. Arsenault socially. His wife worked for Loren years ago. Every time you came up in conversation, he would tell me what a talented photographer you are. Why would you be afraid to tell me something like that?"

"That's one of the big questions, isn't it?" I asked, looking down at my barely touched salad. "I've gotten used to keeping things to myself. Things that matter. How I feel, what I care about – those are things that haven't felt safe to share. I know it doesn't make sense."

"Oh, Sweetie, it does make sense. I'm just sorry I couldn't make you feel secure enough to overcome that with me. I don't know everything that you've had to deal with growing up, but I know enough to understand you had to learn to cope with it. And you have admirably. But it's okay to lean on others a little, to share with people who love you."

"It's hard to change."

"Well, speaking of change... Have you made any decisions you want to tell me about?"

I wasn't surprised she had heard already. I'd given the Co-op board my notice. I was going to give my photography a fair shot. If it didn't work out, I could go back to work but this time I would make sure I considered some personal boundaries. I might even go to school. I enjoyed some of the business and accounting work I'd learned at the Co-op. But those were skills that also came in handy as I dreamed about expanding my photography business. The important thing was, I had options. And I had people supporting me in exploring those options.

"I'm going to take a break from work. I'm going to give my photography a chance. But you already knew that, right?"

"Some board members called me. They were alarmed that you were leaving. I know this isn't the full story, but I have to admit, I was a little gratified that they were questioning having put Bill Davis in charge. They were afraid that was why you were leaving."

I smiled at Ruthie. "Maybe I can play up that angle, so they can overthrow him."

"And Anthony?"

I felt my stomach clench. "I don't want to talk about it, Ruthie."

"He cares about you, Willow. He asks about you all the time."

"He does?" My heart rate picked up at the thought. "No, forget I asked that question. I don't want to know."

I spent so much of my time dreaming about Anthony, missing Anthony. I didn't need any new information to feed my preoccupation.

"Yes, Willow, he does. I'm surprised you aren't talking to each other. It doesn't make any sense."

"Ruthie, I know he cared about me. I know he wanted things to be easier for me. But we just don't fit. And he knew that. I finally made it clear enough that he couldn't overlook it anymore. I successfully pushed him away, and I can't ask him yet again to overlook my issues. If he's honest with himself, I'm sure he's relieved he's back to his normal life."

"No, Willow, you're wrong. He's far from happy."

∞∞∞

It was the Friday evening after my last shift at the Co-op. Ruthie's words – *He's far from happy* – had been rolling around in my brain since I'd met with her. I couldn't get the image of an unhappy Anthony out of my head.

Even though Anthony had forced my hand, I'd made some necessary changes in my life. I was leaving the Co-op. I'd encouraged Brendan to step up and take the opportunity to develop a career for himself. I'd told him to seek out a good mentor and stressed that it shouldn't be Bill Davis. I'd developed a full-blown business plan for myself and already had three more galleries willing to show my work. And, probably most importantly, I was open with my parents about my decisions and actions. I made my decisions for myself and tried very hard to not worry about whether they would approve or react. I was allowing myself to be angry with my mom while still figuring out how to love her and have compassion for her at the same time. I had to be finished enabling the dynamics of my parents' relationship and lives.

And I had also decided it was finally time for me to face what Anthony wanted to say to me. I'd waited until this day to do it, and it had come at last. I reached into my desk drawer and pulled out the cream-colored pages. I took a deep breath, unfolded the letter, and sat down, the pain already hitting me upon seeing his handwriting.

Precious Willow,
I'm sorry. I'm sorry for a lot of things, but I'm mostly sorry that I upset you that night, and I'm sorry that I've made you more upset by going against your wishes with your dad. I know it doesn't seem like it since I can't regret either action, but even though I felt I had to do both, I'm always going to be sorry when you're hurt.
You are amazing, Willow. Your quick mind, your

talented eye, your care and compassion, your drive. I especially love those rare moments when you can forget the swirl of what everyone else needs from you. When you're sitting at the lake waiting for nothing more than nature to fill you up and inspire you. I can't look away in those moments.

I wish I could have stayed. I hope you don't think I left in anger. I left because it was too painful to stay. I had become what you hated – someone who loved you and wanted so much more than you were willing to share. I'm no better than that jerk Chris. If I was a better man, I would have stayed just to be your friend.

The fact is I love you. I adore you. And I kept waiting – hoping you could love me back. Love all of me. I've never hoped for that before, so I probably handled it badly. I can only hope that now, by leaving, I've made it easier for you.

Please be kind to yourself. Believe in yourself. Take care of yourself. Be happy.

Love always,
Anthony

I heard Sunshine quietly hop onto the window sill. I saw my shaking hands gripping the letter. I felt the tears on my face and on the pages, smudging Anthony's words. *He loved me? He left because he loved me?* How could I be so stupid? How could I not have told him how I felt? I pushed him away. The person I loved who had been pushed away by the people who were supposed to love him his whole life. I did that. Instead of telling him how much I loved him even though I didn't think he could return my feelings, I kept that love to myself. Tried to preserve what mattered to me. He deserved my vulnerability. He deserved everything I could give him.

I had to talk to him. Now. This instant! I ran to my bag and grabbed my phone. I pulled up his number in my contacts and froze. What was I going to do? Send a lame text? Call him and tell him I loved him and hope he hadn't changed his mind?

He deserved better than all of that. And I couldn't leave him any opportunity to change his mind. I raced to my office to grab my laptop and got to work.

∞∞∞

My nerves were out of control. I stood across the Boston street, looking at the gallery lighting up the December evening. I wasn't nervous about my small corner in the gallery event. I didn't care whether anyone bought my pieces or what they even said about my work. This wasn't business. This was completely personal.

Under my light jacket, I had on a new brown tweed dress. It was probably still too casual for this event, and I wasn't helping matters with my old beloved brown boots, but it was important for me to feel like myself when I did this. I had to offer me as I was.

I was fashionably late, hoping to arrive after Anthony. I looked at the crowd milling about in the small space, shook my hands vigorously to try to release my nervous energy, and began the short walk to what I hoped was my future.

Inside the gallery, I was greeted by the gallery owner. "Willow, I'm so glad you're here. We already have some interest in your collection. And one of the other artists would like to meet you."

"Oh, okay. Sure. Just a few minutes, okay?" I asked distractedly searching the room for a tall, blue-eyed man. When I spotted his form, he was facing my photos in the small corner where they were displayed. His shoulders were stiff, and his hands were in his pockets. He was blessedly alone.

I stepped next to him and adopted his gaze – straight

at the picture of Sunshine peeking out from a tree limb.

"You know what I was thinking of while working on that picture?"

Anthony flinched the tiniest bit, but he didn't turn to look at me.

After a few beats of silence, he let out a long breath and said, "I almost never know what you're thinking."

"I was thinking about yellow running shoes and curious blue eyes. I was thinking about the sound of you jogging away from me that day in the woods. I was thinking about you."

He didn't say anything. He kept looking at the photograph, but I looked at him. At his well-loved profile. At the clenched jaw, the hint of pain and tension around his eye. I turned fully to him and grasped his forearm between both of my hands.

"Anthony, thank you for coming tonight."

"I didn't know about... about this. I thought I was meeting Ruthie. She asked me –"

"I know."

"You do?"

"I do."

"This isn't Ruthie's doing?"

"No, it's mine."

Anthony's head tilted slightly down and toward me. He glanced at me, and I saw his gaping vulnerability. It squeezed my heart and made me want to get everything out as quickly as I could. But there was really only one thing that mattered.

I stepped in front of him and took both of his hands, holding them between us. I lifted my eyes from our laced fingers to his perfect face, took a fortifying breath, and said, "I love you, Anthony."

I watched his face move – confusion, delight, and then his expression settled into doubt. "You're talking about our friendship, right?"

"No, yes. But, no. Let me be very clear. I love you, Anthony. I love all of you. Every part of you. The bossy part, the serious part, the sweet part, the sensitive part, the tough part. All the parts. I love you. I want a future with you. I don't want to spend any more time without you by my side."

Now his expression registered shock. Pure, unadulterated shock. "You're serious?" he asked.

I felt my hopes fall. I knew it was possible – likely even – he wouldn't still feel the same way after all this time. After he'd spilled his feelings, and he hadn't heard anything from me. And it was going to crush me, but he deserved to hear how I felt regardless of whether he felt that way too.

"I'm serious. I understand if you don't feel the way you did. I just want you to know that you are loved. And wanted. You are precious to me, and I want you to know that. I feel that way and have felt that way for a long time. I was afraid to tell you because I didn't think you could ever love me back. But I realize that's not the part that matters. No matter what it cost me, I should have shared with you how much I love you. Because you deserve that. You deserve to know how much you are loved."

Anthony's eyes were glassy, and I reached up to stroke his cheek. "I love you."

He gripped my hand that was touching his face, and he wrapped his other hand around the back of my neck. "And I love you, Willow Miller."

We must have looked ridiculous. Full smiles, teary

eyes fixed on teary eyes. But it was all just background. The murmuring in the gallery. The clinking of glasses and the soft music. It was all just white noise because Anthony was filling every sense I had. Anthony was all that mattered.

"Is Ruthie really coming?" Anthony asked as he stroked my neck.

"No. It was just a story to get you here."

"You know I would have come anyway."

"I wanted to surprise you. She helped, but I didn't need her to actually show up."

"Good. I need you all to myself for a while."

He leaned down to kiss me but stopped just before. "You're sure?" he asked.

I nodded my head vigorously. "I have never been more sure of anything in my life," I whispered.

The kiss was electric, but it was soon interrupted. We couldn't keep ourselves from stopping in between kisses to smile at each other, to say how much we missed each other, how much we loved each other.

But eventually the kiss heated up and took over and Anthony pulled back with intention. "Let's go home,

Kitten."

∞∞∞

Home for tonight wasn't far. It was Anthony's beautiful downtown apartment. It felt just like his cabin, only, here, the modern touches outweighed the rustic ones. It suited him and the city.

"Hungry?" he asked as he took my jacket from me.

"Nope," I said. "Tired." I began walking around his living room, touching lamp shades, curtain edges, trying to muster up my courage. "I think I just want to go to bed," I finally said, leveling my gaze at him.

"Hmm. I think I'm tired too," he said. He stepped behind me and wrapped an arm around me, spreading his hand across my stomach. With his other hand, he shifted my hair to one other side and began planting kisses along my neck.

"I missed you so much, Willow," he said in between kisses. "I didn't think this would ever happen."

I shivered, relished the sensation of his hot breath hitting my neck. I turned toward him, and he wrapped me in his arms fully.

"Have you ever slept with someone when you were in love, Anthony?" I asked as I stroked the back of his hair.

"Yes," he said. I was a little disappointed and told myself it had been stupid to ask the question.

"Willow, I was in love with you every time I was with you. I just couldn't say it because I didn't want to scare you off."

"You were not!" I protested.

"Oh, believe me. I was. But now I can tell you. And that's something I've never done."

He swept me up in his arms and carried me to his bedroom. "Put me down, silly. I'm too heavy."

"Nope," he said as he gently lowered me to his bed. "Can't take the risk of you getting away. I think I'm going to get a guard tomorrow. Lock you inside, so I can have my way with the woman I love for the next ten years or so."

"Only ten?"

"Maybe fifteen."

He kissed my collarbone as he began undoing the buttons on the front of my dress. I was exposed to him before I could process what was happening. His kisses were like a drug. I was dopey and happy and I was reduced to a puddle of feeling.

I began to reciprocate, wanting to feel his skin. I had missed it so much.

He teased me as he kissed up and down my body, saying he needed to make sure I'd been taking care of myself. He examined my fingers, my instep, my waist, and, oh, God, he spent time investigating my thighs and in between them. When I pulled him up to my face, he kissed and kissed me.

"Is this okay?" he asked. He had me pinned under him, my hands held down with his by my head. He was right there, about to push into me – at that point where it felt like neither of us could wait another second. But then he paused. He hesitated until I responded.

"Yes, I'm on the pill. Please, Anthony," I said, desperate for him to keep going.

"You know there's no one for me but you. There hasn't been for a long time." I did know – at least I thought that was true, but I was happy to hear him say it.

"Willlow," he groaned as he finally entered me. He groaned and kissed and stroked. "I love you so much, Willow. You feel so good – I missed this. Missed you."

I squealed and writhed and met his kisses. "Love, love, lo – Oh, Anthony, yes, please."

His face became very serious as he hovered above me. "You make me so happy."

I saw the vulnerability of the boy, felt the need of the man, and I urged him on. "I will always love you, Anthony. There's no stopping it now."

He moaned as he began moving again, and we rose higher and higher together until our love and our need brought us to a peak so momentous it almost hurt.

I lay wrapped up in Anthony's arms after, and we assured each other over and over that this was real. That we were real. I fell asleep and the storms in my dreams were finally gone.

Chapter 21

It didn't take long to blend our lives together. Anthony knew what he wanted. He wanted to be close to Ruthie, and he wanted me to be close to my parents in the place I loved. He was serious about completely diving into his foundation work. His most passionate projects were finding innovative ways to support farmers, helping support music programs for kids, and some experimental work to try to create better experiences for kids growing up in institutions.

If it sounds perfect, it's because it was. For me and for Anthony. He was still bossy and stepped over me sometimes "for my own good." I still overreacted frequently when something came easy because of his money. We knew how to argue, but we really knew how to make up. How to love each other. How to make sure the other one knew.

Anthony found a bigger cabin, and Sunshine and I were moved in. He wouldn't tolerate any argument, and I didn't try to argue much. A cabin in the woods with Anthony? I loved my little cottage, but it lost every day of the week to that. We set up my studio together in one of the spare bedrooms he'd designated for that purpose. He deposited my purple couch in the rustic living room and plopped pillows for Sunshine everywhere. She was living the dream – frequent access to the woods just outside our home and luxury fit for a queen inside.

It was finished enough by New Year's Eve, and Anthony and I were hosting our families for dinner. My mother was doing better. She was at last talking to the doctor now about her issues. I didn't know if she was going to follow through on therapy or on giving her new medication a fair shot, but I was working on letting go a little. I couldn't fix this hard thing she and my dad lived with. But allowing her to take out her issues on me didn't help her. Still, I was a little worried. I always would be when she was going to join a gathering, but I trusted Anthony. I trusted Ruthie and Dr. Marsh. I was trying to live more openly – sharing myself with those I loved. And I was looking forward to our small gathering.

I brought a tray of appetizers from the kitchen to the table in the great room. Anthony was building up the fire. He looked up and smiled as I straightened the place settings on the table.

"Kitten, come here. I have something to give you."

"We don't have time for that, sir." I laughed as I approached him.

"I love having you share your thoughts with me. It's like a whole new window has opened up. Who knew you had such a dirty mind?"

"Enough," I said, playfully slapping his shoulder.

He caught my hand and squeezed it, pulling me onto him as he sat in a nearby overstuffed chair. "My precious Willow," he said as he played with my hair. "I have a gift for you. That's what I meant."

"Anthony! You already gave me my Christmas gifts, and I as I already told you, it was too much!" He'd upgraded my photo printer, presented me with beautiful baubles I would normally never consider buying for myself, and had gotten me top of the line hiking gear. I'd argued and told him it was all too much, but he'd been prepared for the argument. He'd let me know that what he had wanted to do was replace my car and buy my parents a bigger house. I had to ultimately agree with him that if that was where he'd started, he had compromised fairly well.

Holding onto me with one arm, he reached over to the side table for some papers.

"Now don't panic," he said. "I intentionally scheduled the trip for a few months from now. We need to get you a passport, and I would like to spend a little more time here in the woods before we start traveling the world."

"Anthony, I –"

"I'm aware you think it's too much. Willow, I want to give this to you, but, selfishly, I also just want to travel with you. I've been all over the world, but it didn't mean much. To have you with me – to watch you discover things you want to photograph. To watch you eat on the farms in Tuscany and Yorkshire. To get a chance to share new things with you. Please don't say no."

I would have lived happily with Anthony in my little

cottage while still working at the Co-op. I would have lived happily with Anthony even if he still needed to be in Boston. I had to remind myself of that every time his money opened a door that made me uncomfortable. He was able to offer all these spectacular things, but the really important thing was seeing how happy it made him to share it all with me. How happy he was when I relented and enjoyed myself.

"My amazing little man," I said as I traced my fingers over his beloved features. "We'll have to talk to our families about cat sitting."

Epilogue

Anthony

I never thought someone could love me. Really love me. I didn't suffer from some notion that I was an unlovable person. I got along with lots of people. Some of them liked me for my money or for some status thing. But some people seemed to like spending time with me. I had friends. I'd dated several women over the years. Some of them even said they loved me. But I just thought it wasn't in the cards for me. I'm sure it all went back to my childhood, but you can know something in your mind and that doesn't always change how you feel. And I felt like no one would ever *truly* love me.

And now? Now I couldn't imagine life without the force of Willow's love for me. It's like a physical pressure that pushes at me from all sides. And it's the best feeling. For a woman who had tried so hard to turn off her emotions... When she did decide to give in, it turned out she loved hard. And that's what I needed. What I'd been missing.

I was floundering before I had Willow's love – moving from project to project. Achieving. But that was all. The only grounding I'd had in my life until then was my Aunt Ruth, but even that wasn't enough. Wasn't the difference-maker in my life. But on this mournful day when we had to say goodbye to my aunt, I knew this would have been the end of me even trying to reach for something other than what my father had taught me if I hadn't had Willow by my side.

Instead, we cried together, and we laughed together. We had gotten a chance to say goodbye to her and had been as prepared as we could be for this moment. We remembered everything she had been to both of us and felt gratitude for her strength, her kindness, and her will.

It had been Aunt Ruth who'd encouraged me to be patient with Willow. I'd been almost ready to run as soon as I realized I loved her, which was long before

Willow really believed it was. The night she was at the hospital with her mother, I was losing my mind. I didn't know what was happening, but I knew it had to be hard for Willow, and I just wanted to be there for her. And when I had her at my cabin after and understood more about her, it shocked me how much I cared. How much I wanted to fix things for her. How drawn I was to everything she said, everything she did.

She was with Chris, and I'd never loved anyone like that before. I told myself to take things slowly, see what happened. Get to know her. But then when she told me she didn't fall in love – didn't see herself having a long-term future with anyone, I pretended it didn't hurt like hell. I told her I completely understood and went down that path with her. It was Aunt Ruth who talked me down every time I told her I didn't think Willow would ever come around and that it hurt too much the longer I was around her to know she wouldn't ever love me the way I loved her.

Aunt Ruth kept telling me to be patient with her. That waiting for her would be the best thing I ever did. And she was right.

"Anthony?" Willow looked up at me as the service finished. It had been long. So many people had wanted to share stories about Aunt Ruth. The love in the room for her was palpable.

"I'm good, Kitten."

"I would never have found my way to you without her. I wouldn't have known how to love you."

"Do you know how happy this made her? We made her?" I looked down at where I fiddled with Willow's ring finger adorned with my commitment – the ornament much smaller than the one I wanted to give her, but we were learning to compromise.

"I do," she said, meaningfully. "I also know how happy she was to hear something I haven't yet shared with you. I told her before I was certain because I wanted her to know. But I was right."

I looked at her, wondering what she would have told Aunt Ruth in those last moments.

Willow took my hand and placed it gently on her stomach. She covered my hand with hers and rested her head on my shoulder. "Sweet Little Ruthie if it's a girl, yeah?"

About The Author

Arabell Spencer

Arabell Spencer has loved love stories for as long as she can remember. From fairy tales to Jane Austen to contemporary romance – they are all her jam. She hangs out with any and all cats, drinks gallons of coffee, and spends her free time putting herself in situations where she can observe people without having to interact with them.

Books By This Author

Reluctant Bloom

Spruce Lake